Lisa Williamson

Best Friends Forever

illustrated by
Jess Bradley

GUPPY
BOOKS

BIGG SCHOOL: BEST FRIENDS FOREVER
is a GUPPY BOOK

First published in the UK in 2023 by
Guppy Books,
Bracken Hill,
Cotswold Road,
Oxford OX2 9JG

Text copyright © Lisa Williamson
Inside illustrations © Jess Bradley

978 1 913101 558

1 3 5 7 9 10 8 6 4 2

Papers used by Guppy Books are from well-managed
forests and other responsible sources.

MIX
Paper | Supporting
responsible forestry
FSC
www.fsc.org   FSC® C171272

GUPPY PUBLISHING LTD Reg. No. 11565833

A CIP catalogue record for this book is
available from the British Library.

Typeset by Falcon Oast Graphic Art Ltd
Printed and bound in Great Britain by CPI Books Ltd

For Triple Jeopardy
LW

For my Jakey B
JB

Chapter One

Some people don't believe me when I tell them that Evie Peng and I have been best friends forever, but it's totally true – I swear on *both* my cats' lives. Our mums met at a mother and baby group at the community centre. According to them, we were obsessed with each other from the very start.

One of my favourite photos is of the two of us when we were babies. Evie is a teeny tiny thing with rosy cheeks and loads of dark, silky hair. Next to her, I look like a proper chunker with my big, bald head and double chins covered in dribble.

These days though, Evie is the bigger one. In the past year, she's shot up loads, and now, when we stand facing each other, she can rest her chin on the top of my head like it's a shelf.

When we were little, we used to pretend we were sisters, but I'm not sure anyone actually ever believed us. Evie and I might not look all that much alike, but we're the same in lots of other ways – important ways. We finish each other's sentences and laugh at the same stuff, and sometimes, we text each other at the exact same time. Our mums say we're two peas in a pod.

Evie has been in Hong Kong for two weeks visiting her grandparents. The second her plane landed earlier this afternoon, she texted me and asked me to come over.

'Won't she be tired from the long flight?' Mum asked as I put on my trainers.

'Not too tired to see me,' I replied.

'Is that jam on your top?'

I glanced down. There was a red smear on my T-shirt.

'That's not jam, it's blood,' I said, rubbing it with my finger. 'From where I picked my scab.'

Of course, Mum had to make a *huge* thing about it.

'You can't turn up at someone's house covered in blood!' she cried (and *she* calls *me* dramatic).

If I actually thought Evie would be bothered, I'd have gone upstairs and got changed, but I knew she wouldn't. Evie is really neat and tidy (she always makes her bed and folds her pyjamas without being asked), but it never seems to bother her that I'm not.

It usually takes me exactly seven minutes to walk to Evie's house. Today, I was so excited I sprinted the whole way and got there in four minutes flat. I was still panting when Evie's dad opened the door.

'Hello, Lola,' he said.

Before I could gasp out 'hello', Evie came hurtling down the stairs.

'Good grief,' her dad said as we hugged and screamed and jumped around. 'You'd think it had been two years, not two weeks.'

Evie and I ignored him and ran upstairs to her bedroom.

'I missed you *so* much!' I cried, bouncing on her bed. 'I've been bored out my brain all by myself!'

'I missed you too!' Evie replied. 'My cousins are nice and everything, but I'd much rather be hanging out with you.'

'Well, of course you would!' I said. 'Who wouldn't?'

I struck a pose, making Evie giggle.

'Do you want your presents?' she asked.

I let out a squeal. 'Yes please!'

She'd brought back loads of cool stuff for me – stationery, and KitKats in crazy flavours like yuzu and matcha, and a gold waving fortune cat.

'I got one too,' she said when I took it out of its box. 'They're supposed to bring good luck.'

We gave both our cats names. Evie called hers Jiayi, which means 'lucky one' in Chinese and I called mine 'Lionel' because pets with grumpy old men names always make me laugh.

We spent the entire afternoon catching up. After two weeks apart we had a lot to say to each other and didn't stop yapping until Mum called and told me it was time for dinner.

When I got home, a *For Sale* sign had appeared in our front garden.

'Mum!' I called, kicking off my trainers and dashing into the kitchen. 'The sign is up.'

'Brilliant,' Mum said. 'I'd been hoping they'd get round to that.'

Mum and Dad got divorced earlier this year. Dad moved into a little flat of his own while the rest of us (me, Mum and my stinky older brother Matthew) stayed behind. Then a few months ago Mum announced she wanted us to move out too.

The thing is, I don't want a fresh start! I want to stay here, in the house I was born in. I'm not *even* kidding – nearly twelve years ago, Mum gave birth to me in a paddling pool in the conservatory and there's a  really disgusting video to prove it.

Every time I imagine a different family going up and down our stairs, and flushing our loo, and cooking in our kitchen, I get this ache, deep inside my tummy.

'Did Evie have a nice holiday?' Mum asked.

'Uh-huh,' I replied, opening the fridge to see if she'd bought any more chocolate milk (nope). 'Are *we* going to go away on holiday next year?'

'We'll see.'

Humph. I didn't go away this summer. Well, not properly. Now Mum's decided we're moving, she's trying not to spend too much money. We stayed with my boring Auntie Hayley for a week while our house was being painted. It wasn't much of a holiday though. I spent most of it looking after my annoying little cousins who do nothing apart from jump all over me and ask for snacks.

Chapter Two

Two days later, Evie and I went into town to buy some new stationery for school. In just under a week, we'd be starting Year Seven at Henry Bigg Academy.

'I keep dreaming about our first day at school,' Evie said as we walked into Finders Keepers, a really cute stationery and gift shop on the high street and one of our favourite places in the entire world.

'Are they good dreams or bad dreams?' I asked, shaking a snow globe as hard as I could.

'Bad. In the one I had last night, I turned up wearing nothing but a giant-sized school tie. I tried to wrap it around me, but it kept slipping down.'

'I haven't had any dreams,' I said, putting the snow globe down and watching the glitter fall. 'But every time I imagine our first day, I get this sicky feeling in my belly, like I might throw up any second.'

'I know exactly the feeling you mean,' Evie said, linking her arm through mine. 'If only we were in the same tutor group, Lola; I wouldn't be half as nervous then.'

For the very first time ever, Evie and I were going to be in different classes. When they made the announcement at the end of last term, we both spent days crying our eyes out. We begged our parents to ring up the school and ask them to put us in a class together. Mum was a proper meanie and refused.

'It will be good for you to meet some new people,' she said.

I was so cross I didn't speak to her for three whole days. Evie's dad at least tried, but when he spoke to the school, they told him that there was nothing they could do.

Evie and I have made a vow to eat lunch together every single day no matter what. It won't be the same, but we figure it's better than nothing.

We took ages picking out pencil cases. In the end, I went for one with cats on it. I assumed Evie would pick the same one because she's even more cat-mad than me (she's literally obsessed with my cats Twiglet and Tizzy), but she went for a pink leopard print design instead.

We were about to join the queue to pay for them when I spotted a really cute pen with a tiny rubber koala clinging to the top.

'Let's both get one!' I said.

Evie looked at it and chewed her lip.

'What's wrong?' I asked.

'Nothing . . . I just wonder whether it's a bit . . . babyish. You know, for secondary school.'

'It's only a pen,' I pointed out.

And anyway, who cared what people thought?

'I know,' Evie said quickly. 'We don't want to look like babies though, do we?'

'I suppose not.'

I gave the pen one last look before putting it back on the display. *I* thought it was cute.

'Oh, guess what?' Evie said, once we'd paid. 'The house two doors down from mine is for sale. You should buy it!'

What a brilliant idea! I hated the idea of moving house, but I loved the thought of being closer to Evie.

I told Mum about it the second she picked us up.

'Oh, sweetheart,' she said. 'I'll have a look but I'm pretty sure it's going to be out of our budget.'

'What do you mean?'

'Well, when we sell the house, Dad and I will halve the proceeds so we can each buy something of our own. We're probably going to have to move somewhere quite a bit smaller then where we are now.'

'How much smaller?' I asked, panic swooshing around my body. 'Will I still have my own room?' I'd rather eat my own toenails than share a bedroom with Matthew full-time.

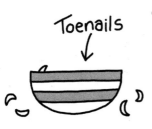

Toenails

'Yes,' Mum said. 'But you need to be prepared for the fact that it might not be quite as big as your room here.'

'We'll still be able to walk to school together, won't we?' Evie said, looking worried.

'Oh, I expect so,' Mum said. 'We're not planning on going far.'

'Good,' Evie and I said in unison.

Being in different classes was quite bad enough.

Back at my house, Evie and I made butterfly cakes and played with Twiglet (Tizzy was hiding) and watched TV. When it was time for bed, we got changed into our pyjamas and brushed our teeth side by side, pulling the ugliest faces we could in the mirror.

After that, we went to my bedroom and played one of our favourite games – *Would You Rather?*

Evie went first.

'OK,' she said. 'Would you rather get married to a zombie or give birth to a zombie?'

'Easy! Get married to a zombie,' I declared.

'But then you'd have to kiss it!'

'Not necessarily.'

'What about "you may now kiss the bride"?'

'It's a suggestion, not an order. And anyway, I could always divorce the zombie straight afterwards. If I'm the zombie's mum, I'm stuck with it for life.'

'It might be cute.'

I pulled a face. I'm not mad about normal human babies, never mind zombie ones.

Brains! Goo goo!

'OK, fine,' Evie said. 'Answer accepted. Your turn.'

'OK,' I said, rubbing my hands together. 'Would you rather eat dog food for the rest of your life, or cat food?'

'Ew! Neither!'

'Oh, come on, you know the rules, you *have* to pick one.'

'Why are your questions always so disgusting though?'

'Because it's more fun that way! Come on, pick one: dog food or cat food?'

'I told you, neither!'

'Evie!' I said in a warning voice. 'You know what happens if you don't answer.'

Yum?

I began to wiggle my fingers. Evie (who is probably the most ticklish person I have ever met) let out a squeal.

'OK, OK!' she cried, scrambling out of arm's reach. 'Dog food!'

'Evie loves dog food, Evie loves dog food!' I chanted.

She grabbed a pillow and chucked it at my head.

I chucked it right back and before we knew it, we were having a full-on pillow fight.

It was cut short by Mum banging on the wall and telling us to go to sleep.

Giggling, Evie and I turned off the light and climbed into bed – me with my head at one end, and Evie with her head at the other (luckily, neither of us have stinky feet).

'Do you think we'll still have sleepovers when

we're grown-ups?' Evie asked as we wriggled about trying to get all nice and comfy under the duvet.

'Of course,' I replied.

'Even when we've got kids and stuff?'

'Sure. Why not?'

'My mum doesn't have sleepovers with any of *her* friends.'

'Well, we'll be different,' I said.

'Right . . .' Evie sounded uncertain though.

I switched on the lamp and sat up. 'How about we make a promise,' I said, 'that we'll always be best friends, no matter what.'

Evie sat up to face me. 'OK,' she said.

'Best friends forever?' I asked, holding out my littlest finger.

Evie hooked her pinkie with mine.

'Best friends forever,' she echoed.

Chapter Three

The night before we started school, Mum sent me up to bed almost straight after dinner.

'But it only just got dark,' I moaned.

'That doesn't matter,' she replied, practically shooing me up the stairs. 'Tomorrow is a big day, and you need to be well rested.'

Well, it was a total waste of time because two whole hours after Mum tucked me in, I was still wide awake. I squeezed my eyes shut and tried to relax all the muscles in my body and make lists in my head – all the usual stuff I did when I couldn't get to sleep – but it was no good; no matter what I did, my brain just wouldn't shut off – all I could think about was school tomorrow.

Back in the spring, we went for a taster day. It was all a bit of a blur, but the one thing I do remember was just how big the place was. Our primary school was tiny, just one class per year group. At Henry Bigg Academy, there are eight! The sixth form girl who showed us around said it wouldn't feel so massive once we'd settled in, but every time I pictured the maze of corridors, I had an army of butterflies flapping around my belly.

Only two other kids from my class at primary school are in my new tutor group – Daniel Littleton, who is super annoying and always calls me stupid names like 'Polly Pocket' and 'Thumbelina', and Serena Salah, who is OK, but not a special friend of mine.

I wondered what the other people in my class were going to be like. Then I wondered if Evie was having trouble sleeping too. If I had my phone with me, I'd message her to ask, but Mum doesn't let me have it in my room overnight. She reckons the blue light does funny things to your brain.

I must have dropped off eventually because the next thing I knew, Mum was in my room hollering that it was time to get up. Twiglet ran in behind her and jumped onto the bed, pawing the duvet as Mum leaned across me to yank open my curtains.

'It's probably best if you have your breakfast, and then get ready,' she said. 'I don't want you spilling cereal down your new uniform.' Why is Mum so obsessed with me spilling things down myself? Whenever we go out for dinner, she always makes me tuck a napkin into my collar like I'm a toddler. It's *so* embarrassing.

I groaned some more, then rolled out of bed, pulled my dressing gown on over my pyjamas and went downstairs.

Matthew was sitting at the kitchen table hunched over his phone. Officially, we're not supposed to have phones at the table, but Matthew gets away with it because he always tells Mum he's checking his homework, and for some reason she believes him.

I was on my second slice of toast when Dad FaceTimed to wish me good luck.

'I still can't believe my little girl is starting big school,' he said.

I rolled my eyes. 'Dad, I'm literally turning twelve a week today.'

'I know, I know. You'll always be my little girl though, even when you're forty-odd.'

Once Dad had stopped being totally cheesy, he asked to speak to Matthew. I slid the phone across the table.

'Morning, Matty,' I heard him say. 'Do me a favour, and look out for your sister today, yeah?'

'Dad,' I groaned. 'I can look after myself.'

'Says the girl who's afraid of the dark,' Matthew hooted.

'Am not!'

'Then why do you still have to have the landing light on at night?'

'In case I need a wee!'

'Whatever you say, wet wipe.'

'OK, OK,' Mum said. 'That's quite enough.'

Matthew is such a pain. He thinks he's the boss of me just because he's three years older. We used to get on, but ever since he became a terrible teenager he's mean and moody all the time. Mum says he has loads of hormones flying around his body and that I should try to be more patient with him, but that's pretty much impossible when he goes out of his way to wind me up.

Once I was dressed and ready, Mum insisted on taking a bunch of photos of me in my uniform.

'You're not going to put them on Facebook, are you?' I asked as Mum snapped away.

'Well, I was going to. Why?'

'I look ridiculous.'

She tutted. 'Don't be silly. You look great.'

I held my arms out in front of me. The blazer sleeves were so long, I could only just see the tips of my fingers, and that was with me really stretching!

'It's a bit on the large size perhaps,' Mum

19

said, adjusting the shoulders. 'But you'll soon grow into it. Better too big than too small.'

When I arrived at Evie's house, she was posing for a photo on the front doorstep. I was secretly hoping her uniform would be way too big as well, but it fitted perfectly.

Evie's mum took a photo of the two of us together.

'Say "Big School"!' she said.

'Big school!' we echoed.

My massive blazer looked even sillier in the photo than it did in real life. Next to me, Evie looked all polished and shiny – like a kid from one of those 'back to school' adverts that had been on the TV all summer.

Evie and I put our backpacks on our shoulders and set off. Almost straightaway, Evie went silent. One of the biggest differences between us is how we act when we get nervous – Evie goes as quiet as a mouse, and I can't shut up. By the time we got to school twenty minutes later, I hadn't stopped talking once and Evie had barely said a single word.

We walked slowly up to the gates, which were swarming with hundreds of kids wearing navy blue blazers like ours. Some of them looked really grown up. One boy even had a moustache! It looked like a big hairy caterpillar was taking a nap on his upper lip.

I pointed it out to Evie, but she was too busy looking terrified to really react.

'Come on, all Year Sevens have to go to assembly,' I said, sounding way more confident than I felt inside. 'Let's go find the hall.'

As we walked up the driveway, a group of older girls pointed at Evie and me.

'Aw!' they chorused. 'So cute!'

'We're not puppy dogs,' I muttered under my breath.

Evie didn't say anything; she just acted like she hadn't heard, but I reckon she must have because her face went as red as a tomato.

We followed the signs towards the main hall.

There were so many different buildings – some old and some new. The main hall was in the old part of the school and was easily ten times bigger than the hall at our primary school. At the front there was a big wooden stage framed by blue velvet curtains, and rows and rows of plastic chairs that seemed to go on for ever.

Evie and I slipped into a couple of seats in the third row. Evie faced the front, her hands placed neatly in her lap, but I twisted right around so I could get a good look at all the other Year Sevens as they filed in.

A few of them were small, like me, but not all that many. I sighed. I really hoped I wouldn't be the very smallest. Back at primary school, I didn't mind being the smallest in my year, because at least I wasn't the smallest in the entire school, but that could easily be different here.

Once everyone was sitting down, the head teacher, Mrs Beard, got up on the stage. She gave a speech about how happy she was to welcome us to the school and what an exciting year we were going to have. Then she handed over to the Head of Year Seven, so we could be split off into our different tutor groups.

I glanced at Evie. She looked like she was about to throw up all over the row of kids in front of us. I reached for her hand and gave it a really big squeeze.

Evie's tutor group, 7M, was the first to be announced. Their form tutor was young and pretty and smiley. I guessed she must teach PE or dance or something like that because she was dressed in a tracksuit and trainers and wore her hair in a high ponytail.

'Good luck,' I whispered in Evie's ear.

She gave me a shaky smile before getting up and making her way over to her group.

My tutor group, of course, was the very last one to be announced. I was hoping I'd get a cool form tutor like Evie, but ours was anything but! His name was Mr Grimshaw and he was even older than my dad. He was bald and grumpy-looking and he was wearing a super ugly poo-brown suit.

As he did a headcount, I felt a sharp tug on my ponytail. I spun around. Daniel Littleton was grinning at me.

'Hey, shrimp,' he said. 'Good summer?'

'Don't call me that,' I hissed.

'Whatever you say . . . shrimplet!'

Ugh, he's *so* annoying!

Mr Grimshaw motioned for us to follow him. As we walked, I tried my best to memorise the way, but all the corridors looked pretty much identical, and I soon lost track.

'We should drop breadcrumbs,' I said to the girl walking behind me who looked like she might be friendly.

'Why?' she asked, frowning.

'To help us find our way back.'

She continued to stare at me blankly.

'You know, like in *Hansel and Gretel*,' I added.

I waited for her to laugh or smile, but instead she looked at me like I had two heads before hurrying to catch up with the girl in front.

I missed Evie even more. *She* would have got it.

⭐

When we reached our classroom, Mr Grimshaw dumped his battered leather bag on his chair and told everyone to find a seat. I hesitated, unsure where to go. I looked around for Serena, but she was already sitting with a girl I didn't recognise. There was a seat free next to Daniel, but no way was I going to sit next to him. I spotted an empty desk by the window and started to make my way towards it, but at the last second, a boy with spiky blond hair pushed in front of me and grabbed it for himself and his friend.

Before I knew it, every single person in the class had found somewhere to sit apart from me.

'You there, the girl with the red backpack,' Mr Grimshaw said.

Me? I turned around to face him.

'There's a spare seat over here.'

I looked to where he was pointing. It was the seat next to Daniel.

I stayed exactly where I was.

'Come along,' Mr Grimshaw said, tapping his foot. 'I haven't got all day.'

I took one last look around the classroom, just

in case another seat had magically appeared since I last checked, before slowly making my way over to where Daniel was sitting. What a disaster!

'You can't keep away from me, munchkin!' he whispered as I slumped into my seat. 'Hey, do you want to hear a joke?'

'No, thanks.'

'It's a good one, I promise! What do short people call miniature golf?'

'Golf,' I replied in a bored voice (when it comes to short people jokes, I've heard them all).

'Well, of course *you'd* know *that*,' Daniel said.

I turned to face him.

'Do you know what we call actual golf?' I asked.

He frowned. 'No. What?'

'*Giant* golf.'

Daniel looked pretty annoyed at that, which served him right!

Mr Grimshaw told us to settle down and handed out copies of our timetable and a map of the school.

'For this week, a teacher will walk with you

between your lessons, but after that, you're on your own, so make sure you pay attention!' Mr Grimshaw said.

Unlike at primary school, where we had all our lessons in the same classroom, at secondary school each lesson is in a totally different room.

I looked down at the map in my hands and swallowed hard.

Chapter Four

As we headed to our first proper lesson –
English – I made sure to keep up with Mr
Grimshaw so that I didn't make the same mistake
and get stuck next to Daniel *again*.

I ended up sharing a big desk with two girls
who were both called Alice.

'I'm Alice Billings,' said the first Alice.

'And I'm Alice Leonidas,' said the other one.

'We're best friends,' they said in unison.

'How long have you been best friends?' I
asked.

'Since reception,' Alice L said.

'I've known my best friend since I was a baby,' I said.

'Where is she?' Alice B asked, looking around.

'She's in 7M.'

'Oh, that's too bad,' Alice L said. 'I don't know what I'd do if I wasn't in a class with Alice.'

'You're really lucky,' I said.

'We know,' they replied, smiling smugly at one another.

I was so jealous! Why should they get to be in the same class when Evie and I had been separated? It wasn't fair! I bet when I told Evie, she would be cross too.

At break-time, we were sent out into the courtyard. I looked around for Evie, but it was really busy, and I couldn't see her anywhere, so I stood with the Alices while they shared a chocolate bar from the tuck shop and chattered away about what they got up to during the summer holidays.

Then our final lesson before lunch was maths. The teacher made us sit in alphabetical order, which meant I wound up next to Daniel *again*!

Luckily, Mrs Helms was really strict and made us work in silence so at least I didn't have to listen to any more of Daniel's stupid jokes.

At lunchtime, Evie and I had arranged to meet outside the canteen. We're not supposed to run in the corridors, but I was so excited to see her, I couldn't help but run the whole way. When I arrived, she was already there waiting for me, and looked totally different to how she had this morning – a big smile on her face.

'How was your morning?' I asked as we grabbed trays and joined the back of the queue.

'So good!' she replied. 'We have the coolest form tutor. Her name is Ms Martinez and before she was a dance teacher, she was a professional dancer. She even went on tour with Little Mix!'

'Wow.' That sounded so cool. The most interesting thing about Mr Grimshaw was the fact he'd been a physics teacher at Henry Bigg Academy for nearly thirty-eight years, and I wasn't sure *that* was anything to boast about.

'I think I made a friend too,' Evie added excitedly.

'You did?'

'Uh-huh! Her name's Cleo and she is *so* nice! We sat next to each other in history just now and we're going to sit next to each other in science after lunch.'

A picture of Evie laughing and joking with someone who wasn't me popped into my head. I didn't like it one bit!

'How about you?' she asked.

I did my best to push aside how jealous I felt as I told her about the Alices, and getting stuck next to Daniel in tutor time *and* maths.

'I didn't know it was possible, but I think he got even more annoying over the holidays,' I said.

'Poor you,' Evie replied, giving me a sympathetic pat on the shoulder. 'Daniel Littleton is the *worst.*'

The canteen was loud and busy, and the dinner ladies were all really bad-tempered, huffing and puffing if you didn't know exactly what you wanted right away. The food looked quite nice though, especially the puddings. Evie and I both went for lasagne and peas, followed by chocolate sponge smothered in chocolate custard.

Once we'd sat down, we compared our timetables.

'Look, we have PE together!' Evie said happily. 'Last period on Friday.'

'Yay!' I cried.

PE's my best subject. I may be small, but I'm fast. At primary school, Mr Riley used to call me Sonic.

'Promise you'll be my partner,' I said, taking

a massive bite of my chocolate sponge – it was just as chocolatey and delicious as it looked.

'Duh,' Evie said. 'As if I'd be anyone else's.'

Maybe things were going to be OK after all.

By the time 3.30 p.m. rolled around, my brain was aching from all the new names and subjects and teachers and classrooms, and my back hurt because of all the new exercise books I had to lug around.

When I got home, the first thing I did was tear off my uniform and get changed into tracksuit bottoms and a T-shirt. I was watching TV when Mum got home from work. As a special treat, she'd picked up fish and chips.

While we were eating, I showed her my timetable and told her about learning the days of the week in French, and the chocolate sponge with chocolate custard, and the fact that Evie's form tutor used to be a dancer for Little Mix.

When she asked Matthew about his day, he just grunted and asked if there were any more chips. Apart from one quick glimpse in the corridor, I barely saw him. Not that I was complaining — I'd happily go a whole year without seeing Matthew.

'Guess what else,' I said. 'Daniel Littleton is wearing Matthew's old blazer!'

'Is he?' Mum said.

In maths, when Daniel took his blazer off and

hung it on the back of his seat, I saw Matthew's name printed on the label.

'Goodness, what a coincidence,' Mum said. 'I gave it to the second-hand shop months ago.'

'Why didn't he just buy a new one?' I asked.

'They're expensive.'

'Yeah, but now Daniel's stuck wearing Matthew's stinky old one.'

'Who are you calling stinky?' Matthew demanded, pointing his fork at me.

'Well, there's only one stinker at the table so you work it out,' I replied.

'All right, all right,' Mum said. 'That's quite enough of that.'

'Yeah, *Lola*,' Matthew said with a smirk.

Ugh, he's so annoying sometimes it makes my blood boil!

'Well, aren't either of you going to ask about *my* day?' Mum said as I scowled at Matthew across the table.

Matthew turned to her.

'How was your day, *Mother*?' he asked in a posh voice.

'It was very good actually, Matty, thank you

for asking. I spoke to the estate agent, and he's already had some interest in the house.'

I dropped my fork.

'Already?' I yelped as it landed on my plate with a clatter. 'But the sign only went up last week.'

'I know. Exciting, eh?'

Was she mad? This was the exact opposite of exciting. This was *awful*!

'If all goes well, we could be in the new place by Christmas,' she added.

'Christmas?' I cried. 'But I want to have Christmas at home!'

'You'll be at home,' Mum pointed out in this overly cheerful voice she only ever uses when she's trying to fool us into thinking everything is OK when it most definitely isn't.

'I meant here,' I growled.

Mum sighed. 'Listen, I'm going to miss this house too, and if I could afford to keep it on, I would, but I can't.'

'You could if you let Dad move back in.'

Mum looked at me. 'That's not an option, sweetheart.'

'Why not?'

'It just isn't.'

'That's not a proper answer.'

'Well, it's the truth. Now, eat up.'

I pushed my plate away even though I still had half a battered sausage left (and I *love* battered sausages).

'I've lost my appetite,' I said and stamped upstairs, slamming my bedroom door behind me so hard my waving fortune cat toppled off my shelf and landed on the carpet. I put it back, then threw myself face down on the bed and burst into hot, angry tears.

Mum pretends to be nice and reasonable, but it's all a trick because she's actually really selfish. She makes out like she and Dad both wanted to split up, but I know for a fact this isn't true. The night before he moved out, Dad came into my bedroom when he thought I was asleep and sat on the floor and cried his eyes out. I bet if Mum told him she'd changed her mind, he'd come back in a heartbeat. If she wanted it to, life could go back to normal tomorrow. She doesn't care about me being happy, or Dad; all she cares about is herself.

At least I've got Evie. No matter what happens, I know she'll always be there for me.

Chapter Five

By Thursday, I was just about getting the hang of finding my way around school. I was excited to see Evie at lunch because during geography, I'd thought up a really good, really disgusting *Would You Rather?* question and I couldn't wait to see her face when I asked it.

When I got to the canteen, Evie was waiting for me there as usual, only today she wasn't alone – she was standing with an older girl I didn't recognize. The girl was tall with tanned skin and big brown eyes and long dark hair tied up in a pony tail.

'Hey, Lola,' Evie said breathlessly. 'This is Cleo. Cleo, this is Lola.'

Hang on a second, *this* was Cleo? I thought this girl was in Year Nine at least!

'Hi,' Cleo said, glancing me up and down.

'Hi,' I replied.

'Cleo's going to have lunch with us,' Evie explained.

Once I'd gotten over my surprise that Cleo was eleven, like us, I was pretty annoyed. What about mine and Evie's deal to always eat lunch together? Inviting random people to join us was definitely not part of that plan! I couldn't exactly say that though – not with Cleo standing right there.

The entire time we were queuing up for our food, she totally ignored me and rabbited on to Evie about some stupid TV dating show she liked. I mean, how boring can you get? I kept trying to catch Evie's eye so I could pull a face and make her laugh, but she was too busy being polite and pretending to be interested.

When I got to the pudding station, I couldn't decide between treacle sponge with custard and chocolate cornflake cake. I was about to ask Evie what she was going to choose, when Cleo leaned across me and reached for a bowl of fruit. I watched as Evie hesitated before putting a bowl of fruit on her tray too, even though it was mostly melon and I know for a fact that Evie *hates* melon.

'Aren't you getting a proper pudding?' I asked.

'Not today,' Evie said, not quite meeting my eye.

'Why not? It's got custard on it, and you love custard!'

'I'm just not in the mood,' Evie said, looking a bit irritated I was even asking.

'Well, *I'm* having one,' I said, picking out the biggest portion of treacle sponge I could find. There was no way I was having boring old fruit when *this* yumminess was on offer.

Once we'd paid for our food, we looked for somewhere to sit. It was drizzling outside so the canteen was even busier than usual.

'How about there?' I asked, pointing out an empty table near the window.

'Ugh, no way,' Cleo said with a shudder.

'Why not?'

'Duh! We need to be as central as possible.'

'How come?'

She tutted. 'Because only the nerds and losers sit on those window tables. Like her.'

Cleo pointed at a girl with frizzy hair the colour of baked beans who was sitting all alone at a table tucked away in the corner.

'Cleo's got a sister in Year Ten, so she knows these things,' Evie said.

'Year Ten?' I said. 'She must know my brother then.'

'What's his name?' Cleo asked.

'Matthew Kite.'

She wrinkled her nose like she'd smelled something bad. 'Never heard of him.'

'What's your sister's name?'

'Yasmin Bayford,' Cleo replied, tossing her hair over her shoulder. 'Your brother will *definitely* know her. She's like one of the most popular girls in the year.'

I could tell by the way Cleo spoke that she thought that being popular was a pretty big deal.

After lots of weaving in and out following Cleo, we finally found a table that she was willing to be seen sitting at.

'What lesson did you just have, Lola?' Evie asked as we unloaded our trays.

'Geography,' I replied.

'Oh my God, I hate geography,' Cleo said. 'So boring.'

'Me too,' Evie added quickly. '*So* boring.'

'What about when we did that project on Japan in Year Five? You loved that,' I said. We tried sushi and made origami cranes and learned all about ninjas and anime and Mount Fuji.

Evie went a bit red. 'That?' she said, poking at a piece of melon with her fork. 'That was just kiddie stuff.'

'Then how come you still have the collage we made up on your wall?' I asked.

Evie went even redder and widened her eyes as if to say, 'shut up!'.

I was tempted to keep asking questions, but I was worried Evie's head might actually explode if I did, so I just ate my curly fries, leaving Cleo to yap on about her summer holiday to Hawaii.

'Did you see dolphins?' Evie asked.

'Loads,' said Cleo. 'Our hotel was right on the

beach, so I'd watch them swim while I was eating my breakfast on the veranda.'

'Snap,' I said. 'Only it was squirrels not dolphins. And instead of a hotel veranda in Hawaii, it was the view out of my Auntie Hayley's kitchen window in Wales.'

Evie snorted and then looked at Cleo who was studying me carefully.

'Did you not go away this summer then?' Cleo asked.

'Not this year.'

'I was going to say. You don't look like you've been abroad. You're as white as milk!'

'Oh, that wouldn't make a difference,' Evie said. 'Lola can't tan to save her life.'

'Really?' Cleo said, throwing me a pitying glance.

'Yeah. She just goes red and gets loads more freckles,' Evie said, laughing.

Cleo wrinkled her nose. 'Oh God, I would hate that,' she said. 'I can't bear not having a tan.'

How rude! I didn't go around making comments about her long hair and then bang on about how

43

disgusting long hair is! Worst of all, Evie seemed to think it was funny!

I was shovelling down my treacle sponge, when suddenly Cleo leaned over and tapped me on the back of my hand with her spoon.

'FYI,' she said, ignoring my yelp of pain, 'some creepy boy has been staring at you for like the past five minutes.'

'Where?' I asked, twisting around in my seat.

'Over there,' Cleo said. 'The one with the sticky-out teeth.'

Evie peered over her shoulder. 'I think you must mean Daniel,' she said.

'You know him?' Cleo asked, pulling a face.

'He went to our primary school. He's Lola's nemesis.'

'How come?'

'He's always teasing her, making stupid jokes about her height and stuff.'

'Yeah, how short are you exactly, Lola?' Cleo asked.

I sat up a little straighter, the way I always do when someone draws attention to my size.

'Four foot two,' I said.

'Oh my God, that's even diddier than I thought,' Cleo said with a laugh. 'I think my little sister is taller than that and she's only eight!'

As she giggled away, anger bubbled like hot lava in my belly.

'I'm a late bloomer,' I said, turning red. 'I'll catch up eventually.'

'Thank goodness for that,' Cleo said, popping a grape in her mouth.

'Why did you ask Cleo to sit with us today?' I asked Evie as we walked home from school later that day.

'Because I wanted you to meet her. And she really wanted to meet you.'

I pulled a face and snorted. That was not the impression I got at *all*.

'Isn't she pretty?' Evie added.

'She's nothing special,' I said with a shrug.

Evie's eyes widened.

'Are you serious? I think she's the prettiest girl I've ever met in real life.'

'You just think that because she has nice hair. I bet if she shaved her head, she'd actually look really weird and not pretty at all.'

'Why would she shave her head?'

'I'm not saying she would. I'm just saying that if she did, she wouldn't look half as pretty.'

'I don't know,' Evie said. 'I think she probably has one of those faces that can carry off just about anything. After all, her mum *was* a model.'

'Was she?'

'Uh-huh. She was in magazines and everything. And if she grows tall enough, Cleo might be one when she's older too.'

'There's more to being a model than just being tall,' I replied.

'Maybe,' Evie said.

'She's not going to eat with us again, is she?' I asked.

'Perhaps. Why?'

'Well, she wasn't all that friendly. She ignored me half the time, and then she made all those comments about my height!'

'I don't think she meant to be mean,' Evie said confidently. 'In fact, right afterwards, she said you seemed really sweet.'

I wrinkled my nose. I couldn't imagine Cleo

saying that at all!

'What about her friends from primary school?' I asked. 'Doesn't she want to sit with them?'

'That's just it; her best friend emigrated to Australia a few months ago.'

I frowned. I didn't like the sound of this one bit.

'You *have* to ask to see her handwriting,' Evie continued. 'It is *so* nice.'

'Nicer than mine?'

I was joking. My handwriting is really messy. I think it's because I'm left-handed, but Mum says that's not an excuse and I should try harder to be neat.

'Everyone's handwriting is nicer than yours,' Evie replied, and even though it was true, it still sort of stung to hear her say it.

'If I ever get married, I'm definitely going to get Cleo to write the invitations,' she added, a dreamy expression on her face.

The idea of Cleo being given such an important job at Evie's imaginary wedding, made me feel really cross.

Invitation!

You are formally invited to the wedding of Evie and Blaaaarg!

'Do you know someone called Yasmin Bayford?' I asked Matthew later at dinner.

'Yeah. Why? She's an idiot.'

'Matthew!' Mum scolded. 'Idiot' is a banned word in our house, along with 'stupid' and 'shut up'.

'Sorry,' Matthew muttered. 'But she is. She thinks she's God's gift to the universe just because she's OK looking.'

'What does 'God's gift' mean?' I asked.

'It means you think you're better than everyone else,' Mum said, reaching for the salt.

'In that case, it must run in the family,' I grumbled.

I told Mum about Cleo and how annoying she was.

'Perhaps she was just a bit nervous,' Mum said.

'Nervous?' I scoffed. 'I don't think so!'

'You never know! It can be intimidating meeting new people, and nerves come in lots of different shapes and forms.'

I snorted. If Cleo Bayford was intimidated by me, then I was a monkey's uncle!

ook!

Chapter Six

I was hoping it was just a one-off, but on Friday Cleo ate lunch with us *again*, and this time she was even more annoying than she'd been the day before. To make matters worse, Daniel was at the next table and kept pulling faces at me every time I caught his eye. In the end I had to swap seats, so I didn't have to look at him.

Evie was the one who brought up the subject of names.

'Is Cleo short for Cleopatra?' she asked Cleo. 'I've been meaning to ask all week.'

'No, I was christened Cleo,' Cleo replied. 'It means "glory".'

'Evie has two meanings,' Evie said. '"Life" or "breathe".'

Cleo turned to me.

'How about you, Lola? What does your name mean?'

'I haven't got a clue,' I replied.

'I'll look it up,' Cleo said, producing the latest iPhone from her blazer pocket and putting it on her lap, out of sight of any teachers.

She tapped away at the screen for a few seconds before letting out a giggle.

'What is it? What does it say?' I asked.

Cleo cleared her throat.

'*Lola is a girl's name of Spanish origin meaning "Lady of Sorrows".*'

'Let me see,' I said, holding out my hand.

'And risk having my phone confiscated? I don't think so.'

'Then how do I know you're not lying?'

Cleo tutted. 'Why would I lie about something *so* dumb?'

'But are you sure that's what it said?'

'Of course, I'm sure. It was literally there in black and white: Lola means "Lady of Sorrows".'

'Lady of Sorrows,' Evie repeated. 'Do you think your mum and dad knew that was what it meant when they picked it, Lola?'

'I hope not,' I huffed, although I wouldn't put it past Mum.

'Speaking of sorrow,' Cleo said. 'That strange boy is gawping at you again, Lola.'

This time, when I looked over, I caught Daniel staring right at me. He looked surprised for a split-second then stuck out his tongue.

'Ugh, he is such an idiot,' I said, shoving a chip in my mouth.

'He obviously fancies you,' Cleo said.

'I don't think so,' I muttered, screwing up my face.

'Didn't you say that he teases you all the time?'

'Yes.'

'There you go then. It's a well-known fact that 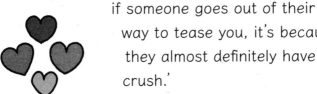 if someone goes out of their way to tease you, it's because they almost definitely have a crush.'

'If it's that well-known, how come I haven't heard of it?' I asked.

'You probably don't have as much experience

with boys as I do,' Cleo said, twirling a lock of shiny hair around her finger.

'Cleo has a boyfriend in Year Eight,' Evie said.

I could tell from the way she spoke that she was impressed.

'He's going to be thirteen in January,' Cleo added proudly.

'I don't think *that's* anything to boast about,' I scoffed. 'Teenage boys are disgusting.'

'Well, *Kieran* isn't,' Cleo said. 'Kieran is very mature for his *age*.'

'Did he tease you before you got together?' Evie wanted to know.

'All the time. That's how I knew he liked me.'

'Well, I think it sounds totally stupid,' I said. 'If you like someone, you should just be nice to them.'

Cleo leaned over and patted me on the back of my hand like I was some stupid little kid.

'You'll understand one day, Lola,' she said.

After we'd eaten, we went to the loos although I was the only one who actually had a wee. Cleo just stood in front of the sinks and put on make-up and pulled pouty faces in the mirror while Evie hovered next to her.

As I washed my hands, Cleo put away her lip gloss and produced a pink heart-shaped glass bottle from her bag. She removed the lid and spritzed perfume on her neck and wrists.

'Ooh, that smells lovely,' Evie said.

'It's my signature scent – Baby Bombshell,' Cleo replied. 'Do you want some?'

'Yes, please,' Evie said, sticking out her wrists.

Cleo sprayed them, then Evie rubbed them together and sniffed.

'Mmmmmm,' she murmured with her eyes closed.

Cleo held up the bottle towards me.

'Lola?'

'No, thanks,' I said, backing away. The smell made me gag.

'Suit yourself,' Cleo said with a shrug, spritzing some more on her neck. 'Oh, by the way,' she said, talking to me through the mirror. 'I asked Yasmin if she knew who your brother was and according to her, he's a massive nerd.'

I thought I'd enjoy hearing someone saying mean things about Matthew, but hearing Cleo say them just made me feel cross.

The last lesson of the day was PE. Evie's class was already there when I walked into the changing rooms.

'I saved you a space,' she said, pointing at the spare peg between her and Cleo.

Cleo had taken off her shirt. She was wearing a proper bra, like the sort my mum wears, with lacy bits and a little bow at the front. I wear white cotton crop tops from the kids department at Marks and Spencer. I got changed really quickly, facing the wall so no one could see how flat I am. Cleo flounced about in just her underwear for absolutely ages, making it totally obvious that she just wanted everyone to look at her. I was secretly pleased when the teacher, Ms Khan, came in and told her to get a move on.

This term, the boys were doing rugby and the girls were doing netball. I was really excited. We

54

have a basketball hoop in our garden and over the summer I'd got pretty good at shooting.

Once everyone was ready, Ms Khan led us up to the netball courts. As we walked, I linked arms with Evie.

'I missed you,' I said.

'But you saw me at lunch,' she replied, laughing.

'So? I still missed you.'

Just then, Cleo appeared on the other side of Evie.

'Have either of you played netball before?' she asked.

Before I got the chance to tell her about all the shooting practice I'd been doing, she started going on about how she did netball at Ferndale (her old primary school) and how she was the best in the class.

'And before you say, it's not just because I'm tall,' she said, flipping her ponytail over her shoulder. 'Although that helps, naturally.'

Ms Khan explained the basic rules of netball then made us do a warm-up. We ran around the court while she shouted out instructions like 'change direction' or 'touch the floor'.

Suddenly, she shouted 'find a partner'. I looked for Evie, but she was right over on the other side of the court and had already been claimed by Cleo. I tried waving to get her attention, but she was too busy laughing at something Cleo had just said.

Just then, the girl from the canteen yesterday, the one with curly red hair, planted herself in front of me.

'Do you need a partner?' she asked.

'Looks like it,' I muttered, watching as Cleo forced Evie to give her a high-five, annoyance bubbling inside me.

'Great!' the girl said. 'I should probably warn you though, I'm *really* bad at this.'

'Netball?'

'Sports in general. I'm Astrid by the way.'

Astrid wasn't exaggerating about being bad at sports. I lost count of how many times she dropped the ball or threw it miles over my head. To be honest though, I was so distracted by what Evie and Cleo were up to, I wasn't all that much better.

At the end of the lesson, Astrid asked if I'd be her partner again next week.

'If I'm not with my best friend,' I said.

Chapter Seven

When I got home from school, I fixed myself a
snack (two digestive biscuits with peanut butter),
then headed upstairs to pack a bag to take to
Dad's. Since he moved out, Matthew and I have
spent every other weekend with him. I miss him
loads in the gaps. Even though we FaceTime lots,
speaking to him through a screen just isn't the
same as seeing him in person.

I was in the living room watching TV when he
rang the doorbell. He still has a set of keys (in
case of an emergency), but he never uses them.

'Hey, Lola Lollipop!' he said when I
opened the door.

I chucked my arms around his waist
and buried my face in his belly. After
a pretty annoying day, it was really good
to see him.

'That's a nice welcome,' he said, laughing as he stroked my hair. 'The white looks good,' he added, nodding at the newly painted walls. 'Fresh.'

Until last month, the hallway walls were a lovely peachy-orange colour. The white feels cold, like a hospital or a dental surgery or something.

'I liked it better before,' I replied.

We had our dinner at IKEA – meatballs for me and Matthew, and fish and chips for Dad. After we'd eaten, we wandered through the showroom and compared which rooms we liked the best. I liked the cosy ones with loads of plants and cushions and bits and bobs. Dad preferred the ones that were simple and sleek. Matthew trailed behind us, his nose buried in his phone.

I helped Dad choose a new coffee table (until now he's been using a cardboard box). Then he let Matthew and me pick out new duvet covers. Matthew picked a super boring navy blue one. I went for one covered with silhouettes of cats.

On the way out, we popped to the Swedish

supermarket and Dad bought me a big bag of
Mini Daim bars. That's one of the very few good
things about Mum and Dad splitting up; he
gets me stuff Mum would never let me have in
a million years – Nesquik and Burger King and
things that could get stuck in my teeth. In fact,
it's maybe the *only* good thing. The worst thing
is living in two different places. When Mum and
Dad split up, they tried to make it sound like
having two homes was going to be really fun and
exciting, but it's not like that at all.

 Dad lives in a flat in a big
modern block on the other
side of town and I hate
it. He hasn't got round
to decorating or buying
much furniture, so it feels
empty and bare. It's also loads smaller than our
house and all the rooms are really narrow and
pokey. Worst of all, there are only two bedrooms,
which means Matthew and I have to share! There
wasn't space for two single beds, so Dad bought
a set of bunk beds instead. When he showed
them to us for the first time, I thought we might

fight over who got the top bunk, but it turned out that Matthew actually wanted the bottom one. I can still smell his stinky farts though.

As soon as we got in, Matthew disappeared off into the bedroom. I helped Dad put the coffee table together, then we watched a few episodes of *Modern Family*. We asked Matthew if he wanted to watch with us too, but he said 'no', just like I knew he would.

'Dad,' I asked after we'd finished the third episode, 'why did you decide to call me Lola?'

'Your mum and I had a shortlist,' he replied, putting down the remote control. 'And when you were born, that was the name that seemed to suit you best.'

'Yes, but how did it make it onto the shortlist in the first place?'

'I don't remember now. I guess we must have both just liked it.'

'So, you don't know what it means then?'

'I must confess, I don't.'

'Lady of Sorrows,' I said miserably.

'Are you sure?'

'Yes!'

The second I'd got the chance, I'd done a Google search and according to all eleven websites I checked, Lola definitely meant 'lady of sorrows', just like Cleo said.

'Sorry, sweetheart,' Dad said, giving me a cuddle. 'I had no idea.'

'What about Mum?'

'You'll have to ask her.'

'Humph.'

'For what it's worth, I think Lola is a very beautiful name.'

'Tell that to the Spanish,' I muttered.

'Tell what to the Spanish?' Matthew asked as he emerged from the bedroom.

'Lola isn't best pleased about the origin of her name,' Dad said.

'Why? What is it?' Matthew asked.

'Mind your own business,' I said through gritted teeth.

Unfortunately, he'd already fished his phone out of his pocket.

'Finally,' he said, after a few seconds of

tapping at the screen. 'An official explanation for why Lola is such a whiny little wet-wipe.'

'Dad!' I shrieked.

'Matthew, apologise,' Dad said.

'Sorry you're such a whiny wet-wipe, Lola,' Matthew said, continuing to tap at his phone. 'OK, so does anyone want to guess what the name Matthew means?'

'Pizza-face?' I said. 'Poo-head? Fart-breath?'

'Well, Matthew was one of Jesus's disciples, so I'm guessing something biblical?' Dad said, ignoring my suggestions.

'Dad is on the right lines,' Matthew said, holding up his phone so we could see what was on the screen:

Matthew: a gift from God

'Yeah right!' I cried. 'More like a *reject* from God!'

Matthew turned to Dad and shook his head.

'I should have known little old Lady of Sorrows wouldn't like it,' he said.

It was times like these that I really wished I

were an only child like Evie. Or better still, Evie was my sister, just like we used to pretend. Her house is only a few miles away, but I always really miss her when I'm at Dad's. It doesn't help that, thanks to Cleo, I feel like I've barely seen her properly all week. Hopefully next week Cleo will make some friends of her own, and things can go back to normal.

Changing a duvet cover turned out to be much harder than it looks when Mum does it.

'Can you help?' I asked Matthew (he was lying on his bunk playing a game on his phone).

'I'm busy,' he replied, not taking his eyes off his phone screen.

Eventually I got the duvet inside the cover and dragged it up to my bunk.

I lay down on my back and looked up at the ceiling. It's a lot lower than the ceilings at home and if I stretch, I can graze it with my fingertips.

I could hear the people in the flat above moving around. I could hear Dad too. He was on the phone in the living room and kept laughing. Whoever he was talking to must have been very funny because he was still chuckling away when I finally dropped off to sleep.

At breakfast, I asked Dad what was so hilarious. It was just the two of us (Matthew was still snoring his head off in bed).

'What do you mean, pumpkin?' Dad asked as he spread marmalade all over his toast.

'Last night on the phone.'

'Oh,' he said. 'I was talking to Uncle Rob.'

I frowned. Uncle Rob is Dad's big brother. He's nice and everything, but he's about as funny as chicken pox.

'What did he say to make you laugh so hard?' I asked.

Dad put down his knife and scratched the back of his head.

'Gosh, I can't remember now. Why? Was I loud?'

'Kind of.'

'Sorry, honey. I'll keep it down next time.'

Because it was my birthday on Monday, Dad said I could pick how we spent the afternoon.

I chose bowling.

When we arrived, the guy behind the counter asked Dad if I needed the

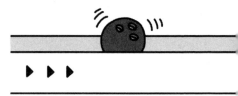

kiddie bumpers up, which was really annoying because if anyone needs the bumpers, it's Dad – pretty much every ball he throws ends up in the gutter.

'Matty, how about we put that away for a bit, huh?' Dad said, pointing at Matthew's phone.

'But I'm in the middle of something.'

'Whatever it is can wait. This is Lola's afternoon, remember?'

Matthew rolled his eyes but did as he'd been told.

As predicted, Dad threw gutter ball after gutter ball and lost both games by miles. Matthew won them both, but I wasn't all that far behind. He still lorded it over me though, beating his chest and strutting around like he was the king of the world.

Afterwards, we had something to eat in the American-themed diner next door. Dad hardly ever cooks when we stay with him. If we don't eat out, we order Domino's or pick up fish and chips. Every other Sunday night Mum asks us what we've eaten and when we tell her, she tuts and shakes her head and mutters stuff about us getting 'rickets' (whatever they are).

We were waiting for our food when a group of teenage girls came in and made a beeline for one of the big booths by the window.

Matthew leaned in.

'You know you were asking about Yasmin Bayford the other day.'

'Yeah?'

'Well, that's her over there.'

'Which one?' I asked, craning my neck to look.

'The one in the middle, taking a selfie.'

As soon as he said it, it was completely obvious which girl was Yasmin; she was the one pouting and tossing her hair about.

'Who are we talking about?' Dad asked far too loudly.

'Shush!' Matthew and I hissed.

'Who are we talking about?' Dad repeated in a comedy whisper.

'Just some stupid girl in my year,' Matthew said (when Mum isn't around, he can get away with saying 'stupid').

'Her sister is in Evie's tutor group,' I added. 'She's eaten lunch with us a couple of times.'

'And do we like her?' Dad asked as the waiter brought over our food.

'Nope,' I said, blowing bubbles through my straw.

'Oh really? Why not?'

'She's a show-off and a know-it-all.'

'Oh dear.'

'Exactly.'

The entire meal, Dad's phone kept buzzing.

'Who's that?' I asked, leaning over to look.

'Just Uncle Rob,' Dad said, turning his phone over so the screen was face-down on the table.

'Again? I thought you spoke to him last night.'

'This is about something different.'

'What?'

'Oh, nothing interesting. You know, just boring grown-up stuff.'

I hate it when adults say things like that. I'd rather they just admitted what they were talking about and let *me* decide if it was boring or not.

Chapter Eight

On Monday, the very first person to wish me a happy birthday was Evie. At 6.12 a.m. (the exact time I was born), she called me up and sang 'Happy Birthday' down the phone. Once I'd hung up, I tried to go back to sleep but I was far too excited. I gave up trying and crossed the landing to Matthew's room.

'What are you doing?' he growled as I jumped on his bed. 'Go away.'

'But it's my birthday!' I cried, bouncing up and down on the mattress.

'So?' he said, shoving me off him and yanking the duvet over his head. 'Buzz off.'

I tried Mum instead. She let me climb under the covers with her and Twiglet (Tizzy, as usual, was cowering under the bed).

'What would you like for breakfast this morning, birthday girl?' she asked as she gave me a cuddle. 'You can have anything you like.'

'A bacon sandwich and hot chocolate?'

'Your wish is my command.'

'Can I have it in bed?'

She laughed. 'Over my dead body.'

'What happened to my wish being your command?'

'I don't care. I only changed your sheets the other day. The last thing I want is you getting ketchup all over them.'

'Really, Mum? Is that really the *very* last thing you want? Out of all the things on planet earth?'

Mum raised an eyebrow. 'It may be your birthday but that doesn't give you a free pass to be cheeky, young lady,' she said, tweaking my nose.

We stayed snuggled in bed for another ten minutes, then Mum got up to get started on breakfast.

In the kitchen, she'd laid out all my cards and presents on the table. While she fried bacon and buttered bread, I arranged them in the order

71

I wanted to open them, working up from the smallest present to the biggest.

The smell of bacon got Matthew up without Mum having to shout at him.

'Aren't you going to wish me a happy birthday?' I asked as he slumped in the chair opposite me.

'Happy birthday, pipsqueak,' he muttered, rubbing the sleep out of his eyes.

I polished off my sandwich then opened my presents. From Mum, I got a board game called Ticket to Ride, a new pair of Converse (hi-tops with tiny rainbows all over them), a lava lamp, a load of stationery and the biggest bar of Dairy Milk I've ever seen. From Grandma Finch, I got some cat slippers and a book token, and from Grandma and Granddad Kite, I got a really ugly tracksuit that Mum says we can take back to the shops and swap for something else.

From Matthew, I got a box of cherry Pop Tarts he bought on Amazon (I love *anything* cherry flavoured).

'Can I have one?' he asked, the second I opened them.

'You can have *half* of one,' I said.

'Half!'

'They are hers, Matthew,' Mum pointed out. 'Just don't eat them all at once, Lola. Those things are absolutely packed with sugar.'

'Yeah, *Lola*,' Matthew said as I ripped open the foil packaging.

I ignored him and took a massive bite.

Not even Matthew being a pain in the bum could put me in a bad mood.

After breakfast, I got ready for school and headed over to Evie's. When I arrived, she sang 'Happy Birthday' again and gave me a card and a massive badge with the words 'Birthday Bestie' on it. She pinned it to my blazer, just above the '12 today' badge Mum got for me, then handed me a small flat box wrapped in stripy paper.

Inside was a really pretty silver bracelet with a charm in the shape of a pea pod hanging from one of the links.

'Peas in a pod!' I cried. 'Like us!'

'Does that mean you like it?' Evie asked as she helped me fasten it.

'Like it?' I said, admiring the way it looked on my wrist. 'I love it!'

In registration, the Alices saw my badge and got Mr Grimshaw to make the entire class sing 'Happy Birthday' to me.

Daniel made sure to sing the wrong lyrics extra loudly:

Happy birthday to you,
I went to the zoo,
You look like a monkey,
And you smell like one too!

'You can talk,' I hissed, once everyone had stopped singing. 'Your breath smells like a ferret died in your mouth!'

'Lucky ferret,' Daniel replied. 'Hey, are you having a party?'

'None of your business.'

'That means you are. And you didn't invite me! I'm hurt.'

He stuck out his lower lip and pretended to sulk.

I rolled my eyes.

'And now I'm going to have to take you off the guest list for *my* birthday party,' he added.

'Oh no,' I said sarcastically. 'I'm *so* sad.'

'You will be. My party is going to be sick! We're gonna go paintballing and go-karting and to the cinema and there's going to be a chocolate fountain bigger than me.'

I frowned.

'Paintballing, go-karting *and* the cinema?' I said.

'Yep.'

'All in one day?'

'That's right.'

I folded my arms across my chest.

'Don't believe you.'

'Fine. Just don't come crying to me when

everyone comes to school talking about how mine was the best birthday party they've ever been to.'

At lunchtime, Evie stuck a candle in my chocolate concrete and pink custard. We couldn't light it because the dinner ladies wouldn't let us borrow a match or a lighter, so we just had to pretend. When Evie told me to make a wish, I closed my eyes and wished for Cleo to leave us alone (she was eating lunch with us *again*!).

'It's so weird that you're the first of us to turn twelve,' Cleo said as I removed the candle and dug into my pudding.

'Why?' I asked.

'Because you're so small,' she replied. 'I bet if you asked anyone which of us three was the oldest, they'd all say me.'

I flushed. 'Not necessarily,' I replied.

 'Oh, come on, Lola,' Cleo said. 'When was the last time *you* were mistaken for fourteen?' She tossed her hair over her shoulder and looked smug.

'Maybe this means that you're going to be all old and wrinkly before the rest of us,' I said.

'Of course not,' she replied, looking irritated. 'It doesn't work that way. You only have to look at my mum – she's forty-five but she looks so much younger.'

Evie told Cleo about my birthday plans – Dad was taking us to an escape room followed by pizza at my favourite Italian restaurant. I'd been excited about it for weeks, but Cleo didn't seem impressed.

'Each to their own, I suppose,' she said, her nose in the air. 'For *my* twelfth birthday, *I'm* going to a spa.'

Cleo didn't have a clue what she was talking about because the escape room was amazing! It was *Alice-in-Wonderland*-themed, and we had to solve loads of different puzzles in order to find Alice and escape.

Afterwards, at the restaurant, Dad let us order pizza and garlic bread and ice cream sundaes, even though we were going to be having cake at home straight afterwards.

When we got home, Dad wasn't going to come inside for a slice, but I begged him and eventually he agreed.

Mum and Dad seemed quite pleased to see each other, hugging 'hello' and asking about one another's days. While Dad got plates down from the cupboard, Mum got the cutlery and some napkins out of the drawer. It was strange seeing them in the same room again; I could almost trick myself into thinking they were still together. I caught Evie's eye and could tell she was thinking the same thing. I swallowed hard and for a few seconds I was scared I might start crying. Evie's hand found mine under the table and gave it a squeeze.

I cheered up when Mum brought out my cake. It was in the shape of a koala and looked really cute.

'Make a wish!' Mum said as I blew out the candles.

This time I made a different wish.

I wish Mum and Dad would get back together.

I stood there looking at the cake. It was so adorable that I felt bad cutting into it.

'Get a move on,' Matthew hollered as I hesitated with the knife. 'I've paused my game for this.'

I glared at him, then whispered a silent 'sorry' to the koala and sliced into the cake. Inside, there were layers of red velvet sponge sandwiched together with cream cheese icing.

I took a massive bite and decided there and then that it was one of the most scrumptious things I had ever tasted.

After Dad had gone home, Evie and I headed upstairs to my room for a bit. We were both in really silly moods, reminiscing about all the funny and gross stuff we used to do when we were little.

'Hey,' Evie said, sitting cross-legged on my bed. 'Do you remember that summer we made coloured water?'

When we were about eight, we discovered that if you coloured in scraps of paper with felt tip pen, then dropped them in glasses of water and stirred, the water would change colour. We spent hours coming up with different colour combinations and taking photos of them all and writing down our findings in a little notebook.

'Of course I do,' I said. 'We thought we were actual scientists or something.'

We both laughed.

'Do you remember what we used to call the black stuff we'd find between our toes?' I asked.

'Sugar dirt!' Evie cried.

I asked her if she still checked for it between her toes and she admitted that she sometimes did.

'Do you think Cleo checks for sugar dirt between *her* toes?' I asked.

Evie giggled. 'I don't think so somehow.'

'No, me neither. I bet she doesn't fart either. Or burp. Or pick her nose. *Or* her scabs! Or even get scabs in the first place. And when she does a poo, it smells of roses.'

Evie giggled so much she fell off the bed.

Take that, Cleo Bayford, I thought. *You may have shiny hair and nice handwriting and a year-round suntan, but no one can make Evie laugh like me.*

So there!

Chapter Nine

My second day as a twelve-year-old was the worst day ever.

Firstly, Mum had to leave early for a work meeting. She woke me up before she left, but I dozed off again, and when I next opened my eyes, it was twenty past eight and I was totally late for school.

As I ran around getting ready, I messaged Evie and told her to go ahead without me.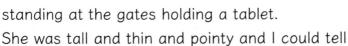

When I finally got to school, all sweaty and out of breath, a teacher I'd never met before was standing at the gates holding a tablet. She was tall and thin and pointy and I could tell just by looking at her that she was going to be super mean.

'You're late,' she barked.

'I know,' I panted.

She narrowed her eyes. 'Don't be smart with me, young lady.'

'I wasn't,' I yelped. 'I was just agreeing with you.'

She narrowed her eyes some more. 'Where's your lanyard?'

I glanced down. I'd left in such a hurry I must have forgotten to put it on.

'I, I don't have it,' I stammered.

'Name and tutor group.'

'Lola Kite, 7G.'

She tapped at her screen. 'Congratulations, Lola Kite, you've just earned yourself *two* conduct marks.'

'But—' I began.

'No buts. Now get yourself to tutor group.'

Mr Grimshaw was halfway through the register when I crept into the classroom. I mouthed 'sorry' at him and slipped into my seat next to Daniel.

'There you are,' Daniel whispered. 'I was starting to worry.'

'Yeah right,' I muttered.

He gasped. 'Munchkin, I can't believe you're doubting me! And after I went to the trouble of writing a poem about you as well . . .'

I ignored him and got my pencil case out.

'Wanna see it?' he asked.

'No, thank you.'

Daniel ignored me and passed me a piece of paper.

> There was a girl called Lola,
> Who drank too much cherry cola,
> She wet her knickers,
> And stained her slippers,
> And ran away to Arizona.

'Lola and Arizona don't even rhyme,' I snapped at him.

'Close enough,' Daniel whispered back.

I got my pencil case out and scribbled on the back of his stupid paper. 'In that case, how's *this* for a poem?' I said, shoving it across the desk.

There was a boy called Dan,
Who had a face like spam,
He smelled like a bin,
And had spots on his chin,
And his brain was the size of a pecan.

Daniel snorted. 'Dan and pecan?' he said. 'That's *way* worse than Lola and Arizona.'

'Are you kidding me? At least mine is a proper rhyme.'

'Lola, can you keep the noise down? I'm trying to concentrate here,' Mr Grimshaw said, looking up from his laptop.

'It wasn't me,' I cried. 'It was Daniel.'

'Then how come I could only hear you?'

'I don't know, do I?' I snapped. 'Maybe you need to get your ears checked.'

Mr Grimshaw's big googly eyes got even bigger and more googly than usual.

'Stay behind after the bell,' he said.

'But that's not fair! *He* started it.' I jabbed my index finger towards Daniel.

'Are you answering back?' Mr Grimshaw demanded.

Why did everyone keep assuming that? First the teacher on the gate, and now Mr Grimshaw!

'No,' I said, anger bubbling in my belly like scalding hot soup. 'I'm trying to tell you what happened. There's a difference.'

'Right, that's it, I'm giving you a conduct mark.'

'But I didn't do anything!'

'I do not want to hear it, Lola Kite,' Mr Grimshaw barked. 'Consider the subject closed.'

I was in a furious mood all morning. It didn't help that in French, when Mr Capron asked me if I had any pets, instead of saying I *have* a cat (*j'ai une chat*), I said '*Je suis une chat*' (I *am* a cat) and loads of people laughed.

I was still fuming when I met Evie outside the canteen. And worst luck, of course Cleo was there too.

'What happened to you this morning?' Evie asked.

'I slept in.'

'Is that why your hair looks like that?' Cleo asked with a giggle.

'Like what?' I asked crossly.

'Like you've been dragged through a hedge backwards!'

She reached into her bag and pulled out a make-up compact. I opened it and peered at my reflection in the heart-shaped mirror. My hair was flat on one side, all mad and bushy on the other.

'When did you last wash it?' Cleo asked, peering at my scalp and grimacing.

'None of your business,' I said, trying to duck away from her.

I turned to Evie and asked for a bobble.

'I have one!' Cleo sang, removing a silky scrunchie from her wrist. 'Just make sure you wash it before giving it back, please. I don't want it making my hair all greasy.'

In the queue, I explained what happened with the teacher at the gates and Mr Grimshaw.

'Fancy getting a detention in your second week,' Cleo said with a giggle.

'Detention? I asked. 'What are you talking about?'

'If you get three conduct points you automatically get a detention,' she replied.

'But it wasn't my fault!'

I expected Evie to take my side, but she just seemed really shocked.

'I can't believe you answered back like that, Lola,' she said, her eyes wide.

I stared at her in surprise.

'I had no choice,' I insisted. 'Mr Grimshaw wasn't listening to me.'

'But if you'd kept quiet and just not said anything, he probably wouldn't have given you the conduct mark.'

'I'm sorry, but Evie's right,' Cleo said primly. 'You were totally out of line, Lola.'

I glared at her. Why was *she* sticking her nosy beak in? This had nothing to do with her!

'Also, I told you so,' she added.

'What are you talking about?'

'Daniel, of course. I told you that he fancied you. I mean, why else would he go to the trouble of writing you poetry?'

'Poetry?' I spluttered.

'Oh my gosh, she's right!' Evie said.

'No, she's not!' I cried. 'In fact, that's just about the most stupid thing I've ever heard!'

 'Uh-oh, we've touched a nerve,' Cleo said with a giggle. 'Maybe Daniel isn't the only one with a crush!'

'What's that supposed to mean?' I turned on Cleo.

'Oh, nothing. I just wonder why you're making such a fuss when you *claim* not to like him.'

'I *don't* like him!'

'OK, Lola,' Cleo said, winking at Evie. 'Whatever you say.'

'But I don't!' I cried.

'Maybe we should talk about something else,' Evie said quickly.

'Sure,' Cleo said brightly. 'If that's OK with Lola?'

'I never wanted to talk about this in the first place,' I growled as the bell sounded for afternoon lessons.

'Excellent,' Cleo said, smiling this sickly-sweet

smile as she tucked her arm through Evie's. 'Then we're all in agreement.'

And at that moment, it became official: I hate Cleo Bayford with all my heart.

Chapter Ten

I was in a furious mood on the walk home from school. Evie assumed it was about my detention, which only made me feel madder. Was it really only yesterday that we were in hysterics together in my room? It felt like weeks ago.

When I got home, I was surprised to see Mum's car in the driveway. She usually doesn't get home until after five o'clock.

'Mum!' I called as I kicked off my shoes.

She didn't reply but I could her moving around upstairs.

I dumped my bag on the floor and headed up to find her. I was almost at the top of the stairs when my bedroom door opened and two men, a woman and two little kids I'd never seen before came out. I stared at them open-mouthed as the two kids ran past me and into Matthew's room.

'Are you looking for your mummy?' one of the men asked. He was wearing a shiny suit and holding a clipboard. I scowled. I hadn't called Mum, 'mummy' since I was about seven. 'If you are, she's downstairs.'

I found Mum in the kitchen.

'What's going on?' I demanded. 'Who are those people?'

'The estate agent is showing a family around the house. Didn't you see my message?'

She pointed at the white board on the fridge.

I'd been in such a hurry to leave that morning that I hadn't seen it.

'How long will they be here?' I asked.

The idea of strangers poking about my bedroom made me feel all strange and unsettled, like I had ants in my pants.

'I don't know,' Mum said.

'Oh, you're no use at all!' I said, stamping out into the garden.

I stayed out there sulking while the family continued to look around.

The kids were really noisy. From where I was hiding on the patio, I could hear their voices floating out of Matthew's open bedroom window.

'*I'm* having this room,' one of them yelled.

'No, *I* am!' the other yelled back. 'I'm older!'

Eventually they came out into the garden and raced over to jump on my old trampoline. I don't think they saw me. I was huddled on one of the patio chairs, my arms wrapped around my bent legs, my chin resting on my knees.

Even though I haven't played on the

trampoline for absolutely ages, watching them leap around on it like it was already theirs made me feel angry and sad at the same time.

A few minutes later, their parents came out into the garden, followed by Mum.

'Are they OK on that?' the woman asked.

'Oh, they're fine,' Mum replied with a wave of her hand. 'My daughter doesn't use it any more. In fact, we'd be happy to leave it behind if you were interested.'

My eyes filled with angry tears. The trampoline had been a birthday present. Surely what happened to it was *my* choice?

'Can I ask what school your daughter goes to?' the woman asked. 'We don't know the area very well so we're still working things like that out.'

'Henry Bigg Academy,' Mum replied.

'Oh. I thought that was a secondary school.'

'It is. Lola's just started in Year Seven.'

'Has she really? Goodness! Sorry, I just assumed she was Finley's age.'

As in the kid on the trampoline? He was eight at the most!

'No, she turned twelve yesterday actually,' Mum said. 'She's just a late bloomer.'

'Oh, bless her cotton socks. That must be so tough, especially in this day and age.'

It drives me mad when people act like being small is something to be pitied or cooed over, especially stupid strangers who are trying to buy my house!

I waited until they'd all gone inside, then I plucked a rock from the rockery and hurled it across the lawn as hard as I could. It bounced, leaving a dent in the grass. It made me feel a tiny bit better, so I threw another rock, and then another. When Mum saw the gaps, she would be mad, but I didn't care. It served her right for ruining my life.

'You're not going to let them buy the house, are you?' I asked Mum once the family had finally left.

'I don't know if they want it yet,' Mum replied. 'They did take some measurements though, so that's a good sign.'

'So, you *are* going to let them have it.'

This day was getting worse by the second. First those stupid conduct marks, then Cleo being an idiot, and now this!

'If they want to buy it, then yes. Why?'

'I didn't like them.'

'Why not? I thought they seemed very nice.'

'Well, *I* didn't.'

Mum let out a big sigh. 'Listen,' she said. 'I know you're not thrilled about the idea of moving, but I promise you, sweetheart, I'm going to find us somewhere you'll love just as much as here, if not more.'

I doubted this. For starters, the new house wouldn't have Dad in it.

'Which reminds me,' Mum continued. 'Do you fancy coming with me to look at some places this weekend?'

'What do you mean? As in houses you might want to buy?'

'Yes. I'd really appreciate your input, Lola,' Mum added when I didn't reply right away. 'It's important to me that I find somewhere we'll *all* be happy. You, me and Matty.'

'What about Twiglet and Tizzy?'

'Them too.'

'Does that mean we won't move anywhere I don't like?'

'Like I said, this is going to be a joint decision.'

'You promise?'

She put her hands on my shoulders and looked me right in the eye.

'I promise.'

That night I took ages to drop off to sleep. All the annoying things from the day kept swirling around in my head and keeping me awake. Worst of all, for maybe the first time ever, I wasn't sure I could talk to Evie about it. I definitely couldn't with Cleo still sniffing around. I only hoped my birthday wishes would kick in soon and things could go back to how they were before.

Chapter Eleven

Mum came up to my room on Wednesday evening practically frothing at the mouth.

'I got a ParentMail,' she said, waggling her phone in my face. 'What's all this about three conduct marks?'

'They weren't my fault,' I said.

Mum put her hands on her hips.

'I was late, which I guess was my fault a little bit, but then Daniel Littleton made up this stupid poem about me, which meant I had to make one up about him, and then Mr Grimshaw told me off for talking which totally wasn't fair because I was only talking because Daniel was being an idiot!'

'Lola, what have I told you about using that word?' Mum said.

'But that's what he is!' I cried.

'I don't want to hear it,' Mum said. 'You're at secondary school now. You need to take more responsibility for your actions. Now you've got a detention!'

'But—' I began.

'No buts, Lola. I don't want any more emails like this, do you understand?'

'Yes,' I mumbled.

It was a waste of time even trying to explain; I should have known Mum wouldn't understand.

Daniel must have somehow managed to find out about my detention because the next morning in registration, it was the first thing he asked about.

'Like *you* care,' I growled. '*You're* the reason I got the stupid detention in the first place.'

'I didn't mean to.'

'Yeah right,' I said, rolling my eyes.

'But I didn't!'

Luckily, that was the moment Mr Grimshaw told us all to be quiet so he could do the register. Daniel ripped a scrap of paper out of

the back of his homework diary and scribbled
something on it before pushing it over to me. In
his spidery handwriting it said *Sorry!* ☺. Without
looking at Daniel, I screwed it up and flicked it
back across the desk.

When the bell rang for home time, instead of
going to meet Evie, I headed over to the learning
support centre for my stupid detention.

On my way, I saw Cleo. She was getting
something out of her locker, and I was hoping I
could slip past her before she saw
me, but at the last second, she
turned around.

'Where are you off to?' she
asked, even though I knew that
she knew I had detention.

'Detention, remember,' I muttered.

'Oh, yes! Poor you. I hope it's not *too* awful.'

She stuck out her lower lip in sympathy, but I
didn't buy it for one measly second.

'I still can't believe you got one in your second
week,' she added with a giggle.

Hatred surged up my legs and into my chest.

'Yeah, well, we can't all be total suck-ups,' I snapped.

And with that, I continued down the corridor, my head held high.

I turned the corner to discover the teacher on duty was the same one who'd given me my first two conduct marks on Tuesday. When she saw me, she pursed her lips together tightly, like she was sucking on a super sour lemon.

'Oh dear,' she said. 'This isn't the best of starts to your Henry Bigg Academy career, is it, Lola Kite?'

'No, miss,' I mumbled.

'Well, let's just hope it's not a sign of things to come, eh?'

'Yes, miss.'

She ushered me into the classroom. There were four people already there – three Years Eights and one Year Seven – and I didn't recognise any of them. I picked a desk near the front, away from them all, and sat down.

I was just getting my pencil case out when I realised someone was standing in front of me.

I looked up. It was Astrid, the girl I'd met in PE the week before.

'Can I sit here?' she asked, pointing at the empty seat to my left.

'I suppose,' I said, moving my stuff.

'Oh my gosh, your pencil case is *adorable*,' she said, plonking herself down next to me.

She picked it up and inspected it closely, cooing over the fluffy zip that looks like a cat's tail.

'Do you have cats?' she asked, putting it down again.

'Two,' I said grumpily.

'Names, please!'

'Twiglet and Tizzy.'

'Cute!'

Why was she talking to me? We were supposed to be being quiet.

'I'm absolutely bonkers about animals,' she continued. 'But we can't have any because my little brother is allergic to pretty much anything with fur.'

'What happens to him?' I couldn't help asking.

'His nose runs, and his eyes get all red and puffy. It's pretty disgusting actually. I've asked for a snake for my birthday, but my mum says they give her the heebie-jeebies.'

'A gecko then?' I suggested.

She let out a heavy sigh. 'Alas, my parents have said no to *all* reptiles. When I'm older I'm going to make up for it though – it'll be like living in a zoo.'

'What's your favourite animal?' I asked.

'Oh, that's easy,' Astrid said. 'A sloth.'

'Sloths are one of my favourites too!'

'Aren't they the best? I love them *so* much. Have you seen that YouTube video of the sloth who is best friends with a beagle? It's the cutest thing ever. Hang on, I'll show you.'

She reached into her blazer pocket for her phone and was searching for the video when the teacher strode into the room.

'Astrid Chaney!' she barked, making us both flinch. 'What on earth do you think you're doing? Phone away, now. And move to a desk of your own. This is detention, not a social gathering.'

Astrid made an 'oops' face and gathered up her things.

'I'll show you later,' she whispered, moving to a desk across the aisle.

Detention wasn't actually all that bad. We just had to sit in silence and do our homework. I looked across the aisle – Astrid was writing furiously, her mass of frizzy hair quivering as her pen moved across the page.

After about half an hour, the teacher gave us a lecture about behaviour and respect and then told us we could go. As Astrid packed up her stuff, one of the bits of paper she'd been writing on floated off the desk and landed on the floor at my feet. I crouched down to pick it up. At the top, in handwriting even messier than mine, it said, *The Legend of Cahearah: Chapter 23.*

I handed it back to her.

'Oh, thanks,' she said, shoving it in her bag.

'Hey, do you wanna see that video now?'

I shrugged. 'Yeah, OK.'

We headed out into the empty courtyard. The school felt different to how it did during the day – quiet and still and a lot less overwhelming. We sat on a bench while Astrid searched for the video on her phone.

'Here you go,' she said, holding it up so I could see.

'Oh my god, they're so cute together!' I said at the end of the clip.

'Isn't it the sweetest thing you've ever seen? I must have watched it at least one hundred times.'

'That's probably the number of times I've watched the video of the cat on a treadmill.'

'Ooh, I don't think I've seen that one.'

We spent the next ten minutes taking it in turns to show one another our favourite cat videos. We were in fits of laughter watching a video where some guy had edited his cat into the film *Titanic* when a caretaker appeared and told us he needed us to leave so he could lock up.

Astrid put her phone away and we started walking towards the gates.

'What was your detention for by the way?' she asked.

I told her about being late and forgetting my lanyard and my argument with Mr Grimshaw.

'That's so unfair,' Astrid said. 'That Daniel boy should have got the conduct mark, not you.'

'Thank you!' I cried. 'Finally, somebody agrees with me!'

'Well, of course I do! It was totally his fault.'

Too bad my best friend doesn't see it that way, I thought.

'What was your detention for?' I asked.

Astrid sighed. 'Writing in lessons.'

'You mean, doing your work?' I asked, confused.

'Not exactly. I got caught writing my novel in maths.'

'You're writing a novel?'

'Uh-huh,' she said, her face lighting up. 'It's the first book in a trilogy I have planned. It's about this girl called Cahearah who finds out that she's actually a warrior princess and has to leave her regular life behind to go defend her ancient tribe.'

'And does she?'

'Of course! I haven't gotten to that bit yet though. At the moment she's still getting to grips with using her chakram.'

'What's that?'

'It's an ancient weapon, this super sharp metal disc that you throw. Kind of like a Frisbee but way deadlier.'

Astrid mimed hurling one through the air.

'I know I probably shouldn't be working on it during lessons,' she said. 'But sometimes, these really great ideas pop into my head, and I just have to get them down on paper before they go away again. The problem is, I keep getting caught. At my old school, the teachers didn't seem to mind so much, but here they go absolutely nuts!'

'Secondary school is quite a bit different to primary, isn't it?' I said.

'You can say that again! Everyone seems to get cross over the slightest little thing.'

It was a relief to hear that someone else was finding Year Seven tricky too.

'Which primary did you go to?' I asked.

'Ferndale.'

'Oh! You must know Cleo Bayford then.'

'Yeah, she was in my class. How do *you* know her?'

'Through my best friend. Did you like her?'

But before Astrid had the chance to reply, a car sounded its horn. She looked over her shoulder.

'My dad,' she said. 'I'd better go. Bye, Lola!'

'Bye,' I said, watching as she hurried across the road, her shoelaces flapping, and dived into the waiting car.

Chapter Twelve

It was Friday, which meant fish and chips for lunch. I was really hungry so I asked the dinner lady for an extra large portion.

'All that greasy food will give you spots,' Cleo said, eyeing my plate as we moved down the serving line.

'I've never had a spot in my life,' I replied.

'Maybe not yet,' Cleo said, reaching for a bowl for her salad. 'But you will when you *finally* go through puberty, especially if you keep eating stuff like that.'

I ignored her and took care to take the biggest slice of jam roly-poly on offer.

Evie didn't get any fish and chips either.

'My tummy hurts,' she said, when I asked her why she was only having a tiny little jacket potato.

'It's a shame they don't do ginger tea here,' Cleo said. 'That's what I always have when I have period cramps.'

I turned to Evie.

'Period cramps?' I said. 'But you don't even get your period.'

'I do now.'

'Since when?'

'Since about seven o'clock this morning.'

'Isn't it exciting?' Cleo said, butting in before I had the chance to respond. 'Honestly, I was *so* excited when you told me, Evie.'

I felt like I'd been punched in the stomach. I knew Evie had always thought that getting her period was a big deal, but I'd never dreamed she'd tell Cleo before sharing the news with me.

'Why didn't you tell me?' I asked her.

'I didn't think you'd be interested,' she replied with a guilty shrug.

'Of course I would!'

Once again, Cleo butted in before Evie could answer me.

109

'I think what Evie is trying to say is that she wanted the first friend she told to be someone who actually understands and can offer advice, and let's face it, Lola, you're not going to get your period for ages.'

'Why not?' I demanded.

Cleo laughed. 'Because you're so little, of course! I bet you won't get yours until you're fifteen at least. I got mine when I was ten,' she added smugly, tossing her hair over her shoulder. 'Then again, I've always been very mature for my age.'

I was so angry I couldn't speak. I didn't care if I didn't get my period until I was twenty-one, I'm Evie's best friend which means she should have told *me* first!

As Cleo and Evie jabbered on about sanitary pads and period pains and hormones, my anger quickly turned to jealousy. I kept telling myself

that periods are yucky and annoying, and I was actually really lucky not to have mine yet, but I couldn't help but feel left out. It was like the two of them had their own special club – one that I had no way of joining, at least not for a while yet.

'We might end up in sync,' Cleo said.

'How do you mean?' Evie asked.

'When *women* spend a lot of time together, their pheromones influence each other and sometimes they end up having their monthly cycle at the same time.'

'Wow, I hope so!' Evie said.

'Are you sure about this?' I asked, screwing up my face. 'Because it sounds totally made up to me.'

'Google it if you like, Lola,' Cleo replied snootily. 'But take it from me, it's scientific fact.'

I was upset all day. Even though Evie kept insisting she only told Cleo first because she assumed I wouldn't care, it still felt like a betrayal.

After dinner, I waited until Matthew had gone upstairs before asking Mum when she got her period.

'I can tell you exactly,' she said as I helped

111

her load the dishwasher. 'It was two days before my fourteenth birthday. I remember because I spent my entire party utterly terrified I was going to bleed on my brand new white jeans.'

She chuckled at the memory.

'Does that mean I'll be fourteen when I get mine?' I asked.

'Not necessarily. It could be earlier, it could be later; everyone's different. Why do you ask?'

'Evie got hers last night,' I said, fiddling with my peas-in-a-pod bracelet.

I didn't realise just how upset I was about it until I heard the wobble in my voice.

Mum put the last plate in the dishwasher.

'How do you feel about it?' she asked.

I shrugged and looked away so she wouldn't see that my eyes were all watery.

'Are you OK, Lola?'

''Course,' I said, putting on a brave face. 'It's just a bit weird, that's all.'

I didn't want to tell her about Evie telling Cleo first; I didn't want to admit it out loud.

'They're overrated, you know,' Mum said, inserting a dishwasher tablet in the slot.

'Periods, I mean. When I was your age, I was obsessed with getting mine, but almost the second it arrived, I struggled to see what all the fuss is about.'

'How come?'

'Oh, my goodness, where do I start?' she said, smiling. 'They're messy, inconvenient, sometimes painful, not to mention expensive. Believe me, Lola, enjoy the fact you don't have to deal with them right now, because once you do, that's it, for the next thirty-odd years of your life.'

I couldn't decide if she was telling the truth or just saying what she thought I wanted to hear.

'Is it true that if you spend a lot of time with a person, you'll get your periods at the same time too?' I asked.

'I'm not sure of the exact science behind it, but it definitely happened with me and my housemates when I was at uni. Why?'

'Oh, nothing,' I sighed, my shoulders slumping in disappointment. 'Just something Cleo said.'

Mum turned the dishwasher on. Within seconds, it was whirring softly.

'Are the two of you getting on any better?' she asked.

'Nope.'

'Oh dear. What's been going on?'

I sighed. 'She's always making these little comments and giving me these funny looks.'

'Maybe she's jealous.'

'Of who?'

'Of you!'

I snorted. 'Yeah, right! She's totally full of herself.'

'It could be an act.'

'I don't think so, Mum. Cleo Bayford is like the most confident person I've ever met. I bet she even snogs the mirror when no one is looking.'

Mum cocked her head to one side.

'Have you ever spent any time together, just the two of you?'

I shook my head hard.

'Well, maybe you should. See what she's all about.'

I tutted. 'I already know what she's about. *Cleo.*'

'Oh, she can't be all that bad. Evie likes her, doesn't she?'

'Yes, but I haven't a clue why! She's *so* boring! All she talks about is boys and make-up and perfume and how great she is at absolutely everything.'

I pretended to flip my hair over my shoulder the way Cleo always does.

'And Evie?' Mum asked gently. 'Is she interested in those things? Boys and make-up?'

'Of course not,' I scoffed.

Evie was interested in all the same stuff *I* was interested in – koalas and cute stationery and silly games and YouTube videos of cats.

Wasn't she?

Chapter Thirteen

On Saturday, Matthew didn't come with Mum and me to look at houses. He said he had too much homework, but I reckon he just wanted to lie in bed in his pants and play video games all day. He told us that so long as there was enough space in his new bedroom for the gaming chair he wants for Christmas, he doesn't care where we live.

Mum had lined up five different houses for us to view and I was ready to hate every single one (or at least pretend I did). In the end though, I didn't have to pretend at all – every place we looked at was awful.

'What's wrong with this one?' Mum asked as we looked around the fifth and final house.

'It's too small,' I replied.

Mum said that was the whole point, and that

moving to a smaller place would force us to have a 'proper clear-out'.

'But I don't want to have a clear-out,' I said.

'Oh, come on, Lola. You've got stuff in your cupboards that you haven't touched in years.'

'That doesn't mean I want to get rid of it.'

'So you're just going to hang on to it for ever, is that what you're telling me?'

'Maybe,' I said, pouting.

We were in the kitchen. It was long and narrow and smelled fusty. A small window looked out onto the back garden, which wasn't really a garden at all – just a little concrete square. I thought of our back garden at home with its nice big lawn and fruit trees and fishpond.

'It'll be great not to have to get the mower out all the time,' Mum said.

'What about Twiglet and Tizzy?' I asked.

During the summer, they liked to stretch out on the grass.

Mum laughed. 'I love those daft cats as much as you do, Lola, but I'm not about to let their sunbathing habits dictate where we live.'

The estate agent, a man wearing a shiny suit and too much hair gel, popped his head around the door.

'So, how do you like this one?' he asked, looking hopeful.

'It's disgusting,' I replied before Mum could answer. I pushed past him and stamped outside.

I sat on the front wall until Mum came out. I could tell she was mad with me because her ears had gone really red.

'There was no need to be so rude, Lola,' she snapped as we walked back to the car.

'I wasn't being rude,' I replied. 'He asked a question, and I answered it.'

'Well, your answer was very rude.'

'It's not like it's *his* house, is it?'

'That's not the point.'

'You don't actually like it, do you?'

'I haven't made any decisions yet, Lola,' Mum said, unlocking the car.

'You promised that we wouldn't move anywhere I didn't like!' I cried, throwing myself into the passenger seat in a strop.

'That was before I realised you'd already made up your mind that you weren't going to like anywhere.'

'That's not true!' I insisted. 'I didn't like any of the places we looked at because they were all terrible!'

'You didn't even give them a chance.'

'Yes, I did. It's not my fault you've got such horrible taste in houses.'

Mum let out an exasperated sigh.

'Lola, you need to understand that we're not going to be able to afford somewhere as big as what you're used to. I wish we could, but we can't, OK?'

'And whose fault is that?'

Mum frowned.

'It's no one's fault, darling. It's just the way things are right now.'

'Well, of course *you'd* say that.'

'What does that mean?'

'Nothing,' I muttered, looking out of the window.

'No, tell me,' Mum said, putting her hand on my arm.

119

'I said it was nothing,' I replied, shaking her off.

She hesitated, then let out another massive sigh and started the engine.

On Monday, I was still in a grump with Mum. I was looking forward to having a good moan about her to Evie, but when I let rip on the walk to school, she didn't really seem to get why I was so upset.

'She promised I'd get a say about where we live,' I cried.

'But it sounds like you were rude about every place you looked at,' Evie replied.

I stopped walking and planted myself in front of her. 'Whose side are you on?'

'It's not about sides, Lola. All I'm saying is, you can't go on pretending to hate every house you see for ever and ever.'

'Who says I can't?' I demanded. 'And anyway, I wasn't pretending.'

I wanted to talk about it some more at lunch, but as usual Cleo totally hijacked the conversation.

'I'm so excited about dance club,' she said as we queued up for our food.

'Me too!' Evie added.

'What are you talking about?' I asked. 'What dance club?'

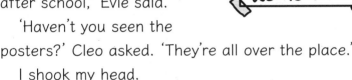

'Ms Martinez is starting a dance club on Wednesdays after school,' Evie said.

'Haven't you seen the posters?' Cleo asked. 'They're all over the place.'

I shook my head.

'I'm guessing it's not really your thing,' Cleo said, looking me up and down, an annoying little smirk on her face.

I was really cross. How dare she decide if something is my thing or not!

'You're wrong actually,' I said, puffing out my chest. 'In fact, I've been meaning to try dancing for a while.'

'You have?' Evie said, looking a bit baffled.

'Yep,' I replied.

'You never said.'

'It never came up.'

'So, you're going to come then?' Cleo asked.

She looked a bit fed up (she'd clearly assumed she was going to get Evie to herself).

'Of course,' I replied. 'I can't wait.'

'Do you have any dance experience?'

'No,' I admitted. 'But I'm a quick learner. And anyway, dancing is just moving your arms and legs about. How hard can it actually be?'

Another annoying little smirk tugged at the corners of Cleo's mouth.

'I guess we'll find out, won't we, Lola?' she said.

On Wednesday, after lessons were finished for the day, we went to the toilets near the main hall and got changed into our dance stuff. I didn't really know what people wore to dance classes, so I was just wearing comfy stuff – trainers, a pair of navy blue leggings and a baggy yellow T-shirt with a picture of a koala riding a unicycle on the front.

Cleo's leggings were skin-tight and had the word 'Pineapple' splashed down each leg.

'Pineapple is the name of a really famous dance studio in London,' she said, when she noticed me looking at them.

She'd teamed them with a matching crop top and a pair of sleek black trainers.

'They're jazz trainers,' she said, arching her foot. 'Especially for dancing in. See the split sole?'

'Have you done lots of dancing then?' I asked.

'Ballet since I was three, and jazz, tap and modern since I was four.'

I could tell she was expecting me to 'ooh' and 'ah' and act all impressed but I didn't want to give her the satisfaction, so I just shrugged and retied my shoelace.

We went into the hall. It was packed. I spotted the Alices, plus a few others from my class too.

'Come on, let's go to the front,' Cleo said bossily, grabbing Evie's arm.

I scurried after them, making sure to insert myself between them so Cleo couldn't hog Evie.

'Are you ready, Lola?' Cleo asked, circling her wrists.

'Totally,' I replied, jumping up and down on the spot. 'Raring to go.'

Ms Martinez welcomed everyone and explained we were going to start with a warm-up.

'Just mirror what I'm doing,' she explained. 'And don't worry if you get lost; it might take a few sessions for the warm-up to sink in.'

She turned on the music and started marching in time with the music – easy! Next, she stepped from side-to-side. This was admittedly a bit trickier (it took me a few beats to get in sync), but perfectly manageable. I glanced across at Evie and she flashed me a massive smile (take *that*, Cleo!). We then added in arms, and shoulders and hips, gradually warming up the entire body, finishing with some stretches. It was true that when I bent over, I couldn't rest my hands flat on the floor like Cleo could, but so far dancing was nowhere near as complicated as she'd made it out to be.

The track ended and Ms Martinez told us

to have some water. While Evie and I were drinking, Cleo slid down into the splits right in front of us. She claimed it was because she needed to stretch a bit more before we started dancing properly, but it was obvious she was just showing off. I ignored her and fiddled with the lid of my water bottle.

After a couple of minutes, Ms Martinez called us back and announced it was time to learn the routine.

She showed us the first few moves. I did my best to copy her, but no matter how hard I concentrated, I just couldn't seem to send the right messages to my arms and legs. I was still trying to figure it out when she added another couple of moves to the sequence. Then, she made us put them all together, slowly at first, then double-time. Within seconds, I was totally lost.

'Having fun, Lola?' Cleo asked.

'Yes, thanks,' I said through gritted teeth as I tried to copy what Ms Martinez was doing.

I glanced across at Evie, hoping she was as lost as me – at least then we could have a giggle about it – but she actually seemed to be keeping up. In fact, the only person in the room who was struggling was me.

We repeated the sequence of moves again and again, but it didn't seem to help – I was more confused than ever.

'Right,' Ms Martinez said, clapping her hands together. 'I want to take a look at how you're all getting on. Let's go in groups of eight.'

She counted out eight people at random.

I was person number eight.

'OK, everyone else make some room!' Ms Martinez called.

'Break a leg,' Cleo said in my ear, then scampered to the side of the hall.

Before I knew what was happening, the music was blasting and Ms Martinez was counting us in: '. . . and five, six, seven, eight!'

I tried to copy the girl in front of me, but I couldn't keep up. When everyone else glided to the left, I stumbled to the right, crashing into the boy next to me and landing on his foot.

'Ow!' he cried.

'Sorry!' I yelped.

After that, my brain went foggy, and stopped moving altogether. My face flaming, I crouched down and pretended to fasten my shoelace until it was all over.

I dared to glance over to where Evie and Cleo were standing. Cleo was laughing her head off. Evie just looked really mortified on my behalf. I couldn't decide which reaction was worse.

The second the music stopped, I fled to the side of the hall. Ms Martinez asked for another eight dancers. Cleo grabbed Evie's hand and skipped forward.

I prayed for her to be awful, but she was really good. She looked like a dancer in a music video, flicking her hair about and pulling loads of faces.

I hate her, I thought as she shimmied and popped and pouted. *I hate her, I hate her, I HATE HER.*

Next to her, Evie was doing a decent job at keeping up. Not only that, she looked like she was having the time of her life, her face lit up by a massive grin.

Unable to stand watching them any longer, I grabbed my water bottle and slipped out into the foyer. Once I was safely on the other side of the door, I peeped through the glass, just in time

to see them finish. There was another round of applause. Cleo held up her hand for a high-five, which Evie returned looking all pink and pleased. I ducked out of sight before either of them saw me.

Chapter Fourteen

Now what? I didn't dare go back into the hall
in case Ms Martinez forced me to do the
dance again. Plus, I couldn't stand the thought
of seeing Cleo's smug, show-offy face. But I
couldn't go home because all of my stuff was still
in there.

Sighing, I meandered down the corridor,
peeking into the empty classrooms and looking
at the displays on the walls and the sports
trophies sitting inside dusty glass cabinets.

I came to a stop outside the library, standing
on my tiptoes to peer through the glass panel in
the door. I was surprised to discover the library
was busy, almost every single table occupied.
A face appeared on the other side of the glass,
making me jump.

The door opened and the owner of the

face – a teacher wearing bright
pink dungarees with a blue
streak slicing through her jet
black hair – stepped out.

'Sorry,' she said. 'I didn't
mean to frighten you. I just
thought you might want to join us.'

'Doing what?' I asked.

'We're the Scribble Society.'

I must have looked confused because the
teacher laughed and said, 'Otherwise known as
Henry Bigg Academy's creative writing club. I'm
Mrs Suleman. And you are?'

'Lola Kite.'

'Very nice to meet you, Lola Kite. Now, what
do you say? Do you fancy giving it a whirl? We
have biscuits!'

I went through my options. I *was* a bit bored
of wandering around the corridors. Plus, Mrs
Suleman seemed pretty nice, and all that
dancing really *had* made me hungry.

'OK then,' I said.

Mrs Suleman smiled and ushered me inside.

The library was really cool. The walls were

decorated with posters and displays, and homemade bunting looped back and forth across the ceiling. In one corner, there was a cosy reading area with beanbags and cushions and squishy chairs. In the other, a metal spiral staircase led up to a mezzanine area lined with computers.

'This is our first session of the term, and we have lots of new members,' Mrs Suleman explained as I helped myself to a custard cream. 'I've given everyone a questionnaire to answer that will hopefully help us all get to know one another a little better.'

She grabbed a pen from the pot on her desk and a blank questionnaire.

'Does anyone not have a partner?' she asked.

A single hand went up and I was really happy when I saw that it belonged to Astrid. She looked pleased to see me too, grinning and waving.

'Excellent, you already know each other,' Mrs Suleman said, walking me over to where Astrid was sitting. 'Now, Lola, you might not have time to answer all the questions so just do what you can. In about ten minutes, we're going to come back together as a group and share what we've found out about our partners.'

I sat down opposite Astrid.

'Why are you dressed like that?' she asked.

I glanced down at my koala T-shirt.

'I'm supposed to be at dance club.'

'Supposed to be?'

'I ran away.'

'Why?'

'Because I was terrible.'

'I bet you weren't as bad as I would be. My brother says I dance like I'm made out of spaghetti.' Astrid waggled her arms and legs, making me giggle.

I sat down and skimmed the questionnaire. There were ten questions in total. I answered them all pretty quickly.

1. If you could go anywhere in the world, where would it be? *Kangaroo Island in Australia*
2. What is your favourite time of year? *Christmas*

3. What is your favourite film? *The Parent Trap*

4. What is your favourite sport to play? *Rounders*

5. Name your three favourite smells: *chocolate, campfires, my cats*

6. Describe the best dessert you've ever had: *a knickerbocker glory on holiday in Spain. It was covered with whipped cream and chocolate sauce and cherries and had a sparkler in the top*

7. What is your favourite word? *Nincompoop*

8. Do you have any hidden talents? *I can talk like Donald Duck*

9. If you were a superhero, what would your superpower be? *Teleportation*

10. If it was raining meatballs, would you eat one? *Yes*

When I was finished, I turned to Astrid so we could discuss our answers.

'Please tell me that Kangaroo Island is *exactly* what it sounds like,' she said.

'Sort of. There are lots of kangaroos there, but the main reason I want to go is to meet the koalas. They're my favourite animal,' I added, showing Astrid the front of my T-shirt.

I leaned over to look at Astrid's answer.

'Transylvania,' I read out. 'Is that a real place?'

'Uh-huh. It's in Romania. I really want to visit Dracula's castle.'

Astrid and I both agreed that teleportation was the best superpower, that we'd definitely eat meatballs if they were falling from the sky, and that Christmas is the best time of year.

'My mum is Christmas crackers,' Astrid said. 'Last year we had *five* Christmas trees. There was even one in the downstairs loo!'

'Wow,' I said. 'We've only ever had one.'

I suppose this year I would have two – one with Mum and one with Dad. I didn't want to focus on that though, so I quickly shoved the thought away.

'What does nincompoop mean?' Astrid asked.

'My dad taught it me. It means "a silly person".'

'In that case, I'm going to use that on my brother the second I get home; he's easily the biggest nincompoop I know.'

Astrid's favourite word was 'serendipity'.

'It's when you find good things without necessarily looking for them,' she explained. 'Like us meeting in detention the other day; that was *total* serendipity.'

Mrs Suleman told us to wrap up our conversations then picked pairs at random to stand up and tell everyone what they'd learned about their partners.

When it was our turn, Astrid got everything about me right and didn't even have to look at my questionnaire once.

'Great attention to detail, Astrid,' Mrs Suleman said. 'One of the most useful skills a writer can have, is the ability to listen and observe.'

135

As Astrid beamed, Mrs Suleman checked her watch and told us that was all we had time for.

'Are you going to come back next week?' Astrid asked as she put away her things.

'I don't know,' I said. 'Maybe.'

We said goodbye to Mrs Suleman and left the library. Dance club must have just finished too because the corridor was full of sweaty people talking excitedly and swigging from water bottles.

I spotted Evie making her way towards me through the crowd, her forehead knitted into a deep frown.

'Where did you go?' she demanded. 'One minute you were there, the next you were gone.'

'I needed the loo and by the time I was done, it didn't seem worth coming back in.'

It was a total fib, but I wasn't about to admit the truth with Cleo standing right there, wearing that snotty smile of hers.

'But you missed learning the second half of the routine,' Evie said.

'No offence,' Cleo chimed in. 'But I'm not sure

Lola ever really learned the *first* half, did you?'
She giggled.

I waited for Evie to tell her off for being mean
the way she usually does when I say something a
bit cruel about someone, but she just continued
to look cross with *me*!

I felt a hand on my arm. It was Astrid.

'My lift's here,' she said softly.

'Oh, OK then. Bye.'

She gave me an awkward little wave and set
off down the corridor.

'How do *you* know Astrid Chaney?' Evie asked
once she was out of earshot.

'I met her in PE. How do you know her?'

'She's in our class.'

This was news to me.

'You're not friends with her, are you?' Cleo
asked. She said 'friends' like it was a dirty
word.

'Well, not exactly,' I said.

'Thank goodness for that.'

'Why?'

'She's *super* weird.'

'Weird in what way?'

'Every way! I went to primary school with her, and she was always doing strange stuff. Like this one time, someone dared her to eat grass and she did!'

'And today,' Evie added breathlessly, 'we saw her talking to a Bunsen burner in science.'

'Are you sure?'

'Cross my heart and hope to die,' Evie said, swiping her finger across her chest. 'She was having a full-on conversation with it.'

'It was *so* odd,' Cleo added, giggling. 'And she didn't even seem all that embarrassed when she realised we'd seen her. She just carried on like we weren't there.'

'Well, she seems pretty nice to me,' I said.

Cleo tutted. 'We never said she wasn't *nice*, Lola. We just said she was *weird*.'

Chapter Fifteen

On Friday, Dad picked up Matthew and me as usual. We stopped for dinner at McDonald's and then popped to the supermarket to get breakfast stuff for the morning.

Matthew stayed in the car on his phone while Dad and I went inside. I was trying to decide whether I was in an orange juice or an apple juice kind of mood when I noticed Daniel pushing a trolley up the aisle. I ducked behind Dad and peered round him.

There were two little girls piled in the trolley, along with all the food and I guessed they were Daniel's identical twin sisters. They were really cute and looked exactly the same, right down to their space buns and matching pink coats with furry hoods. As Daniel steered the trolley past Dad and me (I don't think he saw me), they

were both squealing with laughter.

'First one to spot the strawberry yoghurts gets a ride on the Spin Cycle 3000!' Daniel said.

'Over there! Over there!' both the girls cried, pointing at the yoghurts.

'OK then,' Daniel said. 'Hold on tight.'

The girls clung to the sides of the trolley, screaming in delight as Daniel set it spinning in a circle.

I watched as Daniel steered the trolley over to the yoghurts and lifted up one of the girls so she could reach the ones they wanted from the shelf.

'What's next? What's next?' the girls chanted, jumping up and down in the trolley.

Daniel checked the list in his hand. 'Cheddar cheese,' he said.

'There! There!' the girls squealed, pointing to the end of the aisle.

Dad nudged me and said, 'What a nice big brother.'

I kind of wanted to say, 'Well actually, he's

not nice at all, the opposite in fact,' but I just shrugged and acted like I didn't know what he was talking about.

I stayed hidden behind Dad, only daring to peer over my shoulder once I knew Daniel had passed by. Then I twigged they didn't have a grown-up with them – that they were at the supermarket all by themselves. I was pretty surprised. I'm not sure Mum would trust Matthew with the shopping and he's three whole years older than Daniel.

I wondered what his mum and dad were doing and realised I didn't know all that much about Daniel's family. At primary school his parents never waited at the school gates or came to bake sales or volunteered on school trips, the way lots of the other mums and dads did.

I slipped my hand into Dad's and watched as Daniel and his sisters disappeared from view.

'Who fancies a movie?' Dad asked when we got back to his flat.

'Me!' I said.

'Matty?'

'No, thanks,' Matthew said, disappearing off into the bedroom.

Dad let me pick the film.

'*The Parent Trap*, please,' I said.

'But didn't you watch that a few weeks ago?'

'So?'

'Well, don't you want to watch something new?'

'Nope.'

The Parent Trap is one of mine and Evie's favourite films. We've watched it at least twenty-five times and never, ever get bored of it.

During the film, Dad's phone kept buzzing. Every time he looked at it, he smiled.

'Who's texting you?' I asked.

'Oh, just Uncle Rob.'

'Again?'

'Uh-huh.'

'Is he OK?'

'He's fine. We were, er, just sorting out what to get your gran for her birthday.'

'But that's not until December.'

'I know. We're just trying to be organised for once.'

About halfway through the film, Dad got up to go to the loo. While he was gone, his phone buzzed. I grabbed it. On the screen, there was a message from someone called Kirsty.

I frowned. I didn't know anyone called Kirsty and as far as I knew, neither did Dad.

I punched in his passcode (mine and Matthew's birthdays) so I could investigate further. The phone buzzed and told me to 'try again'. I typed the numbers in again, slower this time, but it still didn't work. Had Dad changed his code without telling me?

I heard the toilet flush and quickly put the phone back where I found it.

'Your phone just buzzed,' I said when Dad came back into the room.

'Thanks, sweetheart,' he replied, reaching for it.

Out of the corner of my eye, I watched as he opened the message, a big smile spreading across his face as he typed a reply.

143

'How was your dumb film?' Matthew asked at bedtime.

'It's not dumb,' I said. 'It's one of the best films ever made. And anyway, how would you know? You've never even seen it.'

'Yes, I have. It's the one about those twins who switch places and try to get their parents back together.'

'Well, you can't have seen it properly then,' I said. 'Because if you had, you'd know how good it is.'

'Here's something I do know – stuff like that doesn't actually happen in real life.'

'What on earth are you talking about? What stuff?'

'People don't go to all the trouble of getting divorced just to get back together again because their meddling kids tricked them into it.'

'Annie and Hallie's parents did,' I said sulkily.

'News flash, dimwit: Annie and Hallie aren't real. Also, their parents got back together because they realised they still loved each other; Annie and Hallie's tricks just helped them figure it out.'

'So?' I exploded. 'It's not like it's impossible! People break up and get back together all the time!'

Before Matthew could see the tears in my eyes, I climbed up onto my bunk. I tried to read my book, but I couldn't concentrate. I knew life wasn't like it was in films, but that didn't mean people couldn't change their minds. I didn't care what Matthew said, there was still time for Mum to figure out she'd made a terrible mistake, I was certain.

After realising I'd read the same paragraph five times, I gave up on my book, shoving it under my pillow.

'Do you know anyone called Kirsty?' I asked Matthew.

'No,' he replied. 'Why?'

'Someone called Kirsty has been texting Dad. I saw her name on his phone.'

'So *that's* what she's called.'

I flopped my body over the side of the bunk

so I was hanging upside
down, like a bat.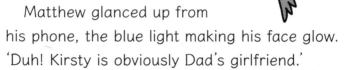

'What do you mean?'
I demanded, pushing my
hair out of my eyes.

Matthew glanced up from
his phone, the blue light making his face glow.
'Duh! Kirsty is obviously Dad's girlfriend.'

I snorted. 'Don't be silly. Of course she isn't.'

Matthew lowered his phone to his chest. 'OK,
then why else does he grin his head off literally
every time he gets a text message?' he asked.

'She's not the only one who texts him. Uncle
Rob has been texting him loads too.'

Matthew rolled his eyes. 'Uncle Rob. Sure.'

'But he has,' I insisted. 'They're planning what
to get Granny for her birthday.'

'You really are dense sometimes, Lola,'
Matthew said.

The blood was starting to rush to my head. I
pulled myself back up then scrambled down the
ladder.

'You've got it all wrong,' I said. 'Dad would never
get together with someone else. He still loves Mum!'

'Well, maybe he doesn't any more. Maybe he's moved on.'

'No,' I said firmly. 'He wouldn't.'

'Then who's Kirsty?'

'She could be anyone,' I cried. 'She could be . . . his dentist!'

'Yeah, right, Lola. Because it's really normal for dentists to text their patients at nine o'clock on a Friday night.'

I didn't have a decent answer to that.

'Face it,' Matthew said, putting on his headphones. 'This isn't one of your dumb movies – Mum and Dad are never getting back together.'

Slowly I climbed back up the ladder to bed. Matthew was wrong, I was certain; Dad would *never* get himself a girlfriend. Yuk, he was too old for a start! Plus, he still loved Mum, I know that he did, I could see it in his eyes. But no matter how many times I told myself all this, my stomach still turned somersaults *every* time the thought of Dad and this *Kirsty* popped into my head.

Chapter Sixteen

On Monday, I got to Evie's house nice and early so I could tell her all about Kirsty, but she didn't seem all that interested, changing the subject almost immediately.

'Matthew was probably just trying to wind you up, you know what he's like,' she said. 'By the way, are you coming to dance club on Wednesday?'

I was pretty hurt. The Kirsty thing had been bothering me all weekend and I'd been relying on Evie to talk it through with me. Instead, she'd brushed it under the carpet like it was totally unimportant.

'Well, are you coming or not?' she said when I didn't reply right away.

'Probably not,' I replied. 'I found it kind of boring to be honest.'

'You missed half the class.'

'Exactly.'

'Whatever,' Evie said with a shrug. 'I'll just go with Cleo.'

The mention of Cleo made the muscles in my neck and shoulders go all tense. I hated the idea of them going to dance club without me, but there was no way I was going to go back and totally embarrass myself again.

'What will you do instead?' Evie asked.

'I might try a different club.'

'Like what?'

'I don't know yet,' I said coldly, knowing full well that I would go back to creative writing club. But why should I tell Evie? She'd only tell Cleo who'd almost definitely make fun of me.

When the bell rang for home time on Wednesday, I headed straight over to the library.

I was trying to decide if it would look greedy if I took more than two biscuits when Astrid appeared at my side.

'Yay! You're here,' she said, grabbing two custard creams and a chocolate digestive. 'Wanna sit together again?'

'Sure,' I said, following her lead and grabbing three biscuits.

We sat at the same desk as last week and ate while the other Scribblers filed in, and Mrs Suleman handed out sheets of lined paper for us to write on. As Astrid took apart her custard cream and nibbled at the custard filling, I wondered if the thing Cleo had said about Astrid eating grass at primary school was true or not.

'Good afternoon, Scribblers,' Mrs Suleman said, clapping her hands together to get our attention. 'As usual, we're going to start the session with a free write. For the next ten minutes, I want you to write down whatever it is that's on your mind. Anything at all! Remember, there's no need to worry about spelling or grammar or anything like that. And I'm not going to ask you to read these out or hand them in either – this is purely an exercise for you. Now, off you go.'

Astrid started writing straightaway.

I picked up my pen and looked down at my empty page.

'Don't overthink it,' Mrs Suleman said as she strolled around the room. 'Just write the first thing that pops into your head and go from there.'

I closed my eyes and waited. The first thing that popped into my head was the 'for sale' sign outside our house. Even though it had been there for weeks now, I still felt a jolt every time I saw it.

I don't want to move, I wrote. *I want to stay where I am and for Dad to move back in and for things to go back to the way they were. And I'm not just talking about stuff at home. I wish Cleo would disappear. She's always sniffing around and getting in the way, and I swear Evie acts differently when she's with her. I wish she'd go make some friends of her own instead of trying to steal mine . . .*

Before I knew it, our time was up, and I was surprised to discover that I'd filled both sides of my A4 piece of paper. I stared down at the jumble of words on the page and tried to decide how I felt. Not better exactly, but there had been something kind of nice about getting everything off my chest.

Mrs Suleman announced that the theme for the week was the five senses. She listed random words and we had to jot down what we thought they might look/smell/taste/feel/sound like. Some were easy, like 'chocolate', but others were a lot harder, like 'moonlight'.

After that, she read a passage describing the smell of bread-and-butter pudding from a book called *Toast*.

'Now, hands up if that made you hungry,' she said, once she'd finished reading.

At least half the hands in the room went up, including mine.

Mrs Suleman grinned. 'Thought so,' she said. 'Now, it's your turn. I want you to think of a smell that connects with a particular memory and write a short passage about it. It could be a food smell, or it could be something totally different; it could even be a smell that's not very nice – it's up to you.'

This time, I knew what I wanted to write about straightaway.

For as long as I can remember, my dad has always used the same shower gel. It comes in a green bottle and smells of mint and tea tree. When I was little, I didn't like it because it tickled my nostrils and reminded me of the stuff my mum put on my cuts and insect bites, but as I got older, I started to like it. Sometimes, I used it when I had a shower. I liked the way it made my skin smell – all fresh and clean. When Dad moved out, Mum stopped buying it. Once, we

went to the supermarket and I slipped a bottle of it in the trolley, but Mum must have noticed because by the time we got to the checkouts, it was gone. I miss the smell, but I miss Dad more.

When our time was up, Mrs Suleman asked us to share what we'd written with our partners.

Astrid went first. Her piece was really funny. It was about the time her little brother wedged a tuna sandwich down the back of a radiator and stank the whole house out.

'Your turn,' she said, when she'd finished.

Even though I'm not a shy person, I felt shy reading my piece to Astrid. The entire time, I hid behind my piece of paper so I wouldn't have to look at her, my face getting redder and redder with every word.

'That was really good,' she said, when I was done.

I had a feeling she was just being nice, but I thanked her anyway.

'When did your dad move out?' she asked as I folded my piece of paper into a fan.

'Just before Easter,' I replied.

The day after he moved out, I ate four Cadbury creme eggs and was sick in the bathroom sink.

'I'm sorry,' Astrid said. 'That must be really tough.'

With hardly any warning, my eyes filled up with tears.

'Oh my gosh, I didn't mean to make you cry,' Astrid said, looking alarmed.

'I'm not,' I said, blinking hard. 'I just didn't

think we were going to have to read our stuff out, that's all . . .'

There was a pause.

'You know, my parents are divorced too,' Astrid said.

I looked up in surprise.

'They are?'

'Uh-huh. It happened quite a long time ago though. I was only three.'

'What was that like?' I asked.

'I can't actually remember all that much. I was confused at first, I think, but after a bit it just felt normal; living half the time with Mum and half the time with Dad.'

'Did you have to move house?' I asked.

She shook her head. 'My mum stayed put, and my dad got a place of his own about five minutes away. They're both my home now.'

I told Astrid about our house being up for sale and how much I hated the idea of having to move out of the only house I'd ever known.

'I'm really sorry, Lola,' she said. 'That sucks.'

And even though it did suck and nothing Astrid could say or do was going to change that, it felt really good to have someone who actually seemed to understand how I was feeling.

At the end of the session, Astrid and I left the library together. Dance club hadn't finished yet. We peered through the glass panel in the double doors. Everyone was performing the routine from last week – the one I couldn't get my head around. Cleo was at the front again, like the total show-off that she is.

'How do you know Cleo and Evie again?' Astrid asked, misting up the glass with her breath and drawing a smiley face.

'I don't really know Cleo,' I said quickly. 'She just tags along with me and Evie sometimes.'

'Oh really? I thought Cleo was Evie's best friend,' Astrid said.

I froze. My heart was beating so hard I swear I could feel it pushing up against the inside of my chest.

'Why did you think that?' I asked, my voice trembling.

''Cause they're always together,' Astrid said. 'And they're always giggling and whispering together and walking around linking arms.'

'That's not true!' I cried, suddenly furious. 'Evie is *my* best friend, not Cleo's. And we've literally been best friends forever, since we were babies, OK?' I didn't mean to sound quite as angry as I did, but I couldn't stop myself.

'OK,' Astrid said, taking a tiny step backwards. 'Sorry, Lola, I didn't know.'

I felt like crying. I knew it wasn't Astrid's fault that Cleo had attached herself to Evie like a blood-sucking leech. But I couldn't believe she thought that they were best friends! That minute, the double doors swung open and people began pouring out, and the next thing I knew, Astrid had gone.

Cleo

Chapter Seventeen

I couldn't stop thinking about what Astrid had said. Just the idea of people seeing Cleo and Evie together and assuming they were best friends made my stomach churn. I knew Cleo was behind it, and the more I thought about it, the more obvious it became that she'd been plotting to steal Evie away from me from the very beginning. Well, she wasn't going to get away with it – not if I could help it!

It was raining on Friday so instead of playing netball outside, we were ushered into the gym for a game of dodgeball. Cleo and Alice L were chosen as team captains. The rest of us gathered in a clump in front of them.

Cleo picked first. 'Evie, of course,' she said, holding out her arms.

I pulled a face as Evie skipped over to join her.

Alice L picked Alice B (surprise, surprise).

I assumed Cleo would pick me next, but she picked some girl called Poppy instead.

I frowned. Literally just the other day at lunch I'd been talking about how I'd been the captain of our primary school's dodgeball team.

I moved closer to the front just in case she hadn't seen me, but she didn't pick me on her next go either, or the one after that. I tried to get Evie's attention, but no matter how hard I stared, she refused to meet my eye.

I started to get more and more annoyed. I'd been letting Cleo tag along with Evie and me for weeks now; the least she could do was pick me for her stupid dodgeball team.

The group waiting to be picked started to thin out. On her next go, Cleo took ages deciding, inspecting each one of us in turn and drumming her fingers on her chin.

'Hurry up, Cleo,' Ms Khan said. 'We haven't got all day.'

'Sorry, miss!' Cleo said cheerfully. 'It's just such a hard choice.'

Her eyes came to rest on me.

Finally!

I got ready to step forward. At the last second, Cleo pointed to the right of me.

'Honor,' she said sweetly.

A girl with her hair in a French plait ran over to join Cleo's team.

I was so angry that I missed Alice L calling my name, only realising I'd been summoned to join her team when Astrid gave me a nudge.

I stomped over to where Alice L's team was gathering and threw Cleo the dirtiest look I could. I sat cross-legged on the floor while Cleo and Alice L finished picking their teams.

There were just two girls left now – a girl called Nell and Astrid. Cleo picked Nell so Astrid ended up with us. If she cared about being the

last one to be picked, she didn't show it. I hadn't
seen her properly since I snapped at her the
other day. As she came over to join our team, I
gave her a cautious little wave. She returned it
with a cheery smile and sat down next to me, so
I figured we might be OK.

We all got into position. Cleo's eyes met mine
and that's when
I knew – I had
to beat her no
matter what.

Ms Khan blew the whistle and off we went.
Astrid was out within the first ten seconds. She
didn't seem to mind, and I quickly worked out
why when she whipped a notebook and pen out
of the pocket of her shorts and sat down on a
PE bench to write.

I ducked and weaved my way around the
court. I was going to make everyone, but
especially Cleo, see what a big mistake she'd
made by not choosing me for her team.

'You're on fire, Lola!' Ms Khan said as I
knocked yet another player out.

Hear that, Cleo?

I grabbed a ball and pelted it as hard as I could, getting yet another player.

Eventually, there were just five of us left in the game – me and a girl called Maya on one team; Cleo, Serena Salah and a girl I didn't know on the other.

Now was the time to bring it – Cleo was going to win over my dead body! She may have had a slightly stronger throw than me, but she was nowhere near as fast at dodging the ball. It was pretty obvious that Cleo was putting all her energy into getting me out, so all I needed to do was avoid getting hit. With every ball I dodged, she was getting more and more frustrated; I could see it in her eyes, the way they flashed every time she missed.

After about another thirty seconds of play, Maya managed to hit Serena, making it two versus two. Then, almost straight away, Cleo hurled the ball at Maya, hitting her in the chest.

Two against one.

On the sidelines, my teammates had begun to chant my name – *Lola! Lola!* Even Astrid had abandoned her writing to join in. Cleo's

162

teammate – the girl I didn't know – was starting to look a bit tired. As she was reaching for one of the game balls, I saw my opportunity and hurled the ball I already had in my arms. It sailed through the air, hitting her on the shoulder.

'Match point!' Ms Khan announced.

Me versus Cleo.

Ms Khan blew her whistle. Cleo lunged for a ball, chucking it at me. I leaped out of the way just in time. Like lightning, I ran after it. I grabbed it, and summoning all the strength and power I had, threw it at Cleo. Time seemed to stand still as it flew through the air, hitting her in the stomach. I'd won!

Egged on by the whoops and cheers of my teammates, I did a victory lap of the gym.

That'll serve her right for not picking me, I thought, as I galloped past the blur of faces. *Maybe next time she'll think twice before underestimating me. And maybe she'll think twice about trying to steal my best friend too!*

It was only when I stopped running that I realised Cleo was on the floor, her hands clutching her belly.

It was so obviously fake, I almost burst out laughing.

'Oh, come on,' I scoffed. 'You're just pretending to be hurt because you lost!'

'OK, Lola, enough of that,' Ms Khan said, crouching down next to Cleo. 'Where does it hurt, Cleo?'

'Really deep inside my tummy,' Cleo moaned, writhing around like an eel. 'I think she might have actually damaged my internal organs.'

'The ball is literally made from foam!' I cried.

'You're really not helping, Lola,' Ms Khan snapped. 'Serena, can you take Cleo up to the nurse, please?'

I watched, disgusted, as Cleo hobbled towards the exit, poor Serena literally having to hold her up.

'Big fat faker,' I muttered under my breath as they passed.

'You haven't congratulated me yet,' I said as Evie and I walked home.

I was skipping along beside her, still on a high.

'What for?' she asked, not even looking at me.

She'd been weird with me ever since we set off.

'My dodgeball triumph of course,' I said, brushing my shoulders.

'Oh, that,' she said in a flat voice. 'Congratulations.'

She managed to make the 'congratulations' sound really sarcastic.

I stopped walking.

'What's wrong?' I asked. 'Aren't you pleased that I won?'

Evie stopped walking too and turned to face me.

'Aren't *you* forgetting that I was on the opposite team?' she asked, folding her arms across her chest.

'So? I'm your best friend. You should support me no matter what.'

165

'I do support you, Lola,' she said impatiently. 'I just . . .'

'You just what?'

She sighed. 'You really hurt her, Lola.'

'Cleo? No, I didn't! She was totally faking.'

'You don't know that.'

'Oh, come on. Our Year One nativity had better acting. And I'm not the only one who thinks it; Astrid said it was really obvious Cleo was pretending.'

Evie narrowed her eyes. 'Astrid? You haven't been hanging around with her again, have you?'

'She goes to creative writing club.'

'Well you've got to be careful! Astrid Chaney is a proper weirdo. When she was in Year Five, she put an actual spell on Cleo!'

'What kind of spell?'

'A witch's spell. She was chanting in this strange language and waving her arms about.'

My lips twitched.

'It's not funny, Lola,' Evie cried. 'Cleo said it was really freaky. And that's not all; Astrid is into loads of other

witchy stuff too. I'm telling you, you need to keep away from her.'

If anything, hearing that Astrid had put a spell on Cleo made me want to hang around with her more, not less.

'It wasn't just that,' Evie added. 'It was the way you were showing off as well. All that running around and shouting and stuff.'

'Showing off?' I spluttered. 'Me?'

I was stunned. How could Evie think *I* was a show-off and Cleo wasn't? It made no sense.

'I wasn't showing off,' I said. 'I was just happy I'd won. And I thought you would be too!'

'Ugh, just forget I said anything,' Evie said, shaking her head.

'How am I supposed to do that?' I demanded. 'My best friend just called me a show-off to my face.'

'Only because you asked! Did you want me to lie to you?'

'No, I wanted you to have my back!'

'Why does it even matter? It was just a stupid game.'

It wasn't though. It was me versus Cleo, and

right now Evie was taking Cleo's side over mine.

We walked in silence for a bit. I had to bite down really hard on my lip to stop myself from crying.

'Are we still best friends?' I asked in a wobbly voice.

'Of course we are,' Evie said irritably.

I'd hoped hearing this would make me feel better, but if anything, it made me feel worse.

Chapter Eighteen

I woke up to the sound of voices outside my bedroom window. I poked my head under the curtains. Two men were in our front garden removing the *For Sale* sign.

My heart leaped. Mum must have changed her mind about selling the house!

I was about to run across the landing to tell Matthew the good news when I saw one of the men reach into the back of his van and pull out a second sign; one with the word *Sold* plastered all over it.

I thundered down the stairs in search of Mum.

'What's all the commotion?' she asked as I ran into the kitchen.

'How could you?' I cried.

'What are you talking about?'

'The sold sign!'

Her face fell.

'I didn't know they were going to do that today, Lola,' she said.

'I don't believe you! And even if I did, you still went behind my back!'

'It was hardly behind your back, sweetheart. I just didn't want to say anything until all the paperwork was in order. Buying and selling houses is a complicated process, it can go on for months and months.'

'Who did you sell it to? That stupid family?'

'Does it matter?'

'Of course it matters!'

I started to cry, hot angry tears rolling down my cheeks.

Mum had the nerve to hold out her arms for a hug. Was she nuts? She was the reason we were moving in the first place; I wouldn't hug her if she were the last person on earth!

I ran back upstairs and flung myself on the bed, sending all my cuddly toys flying.

I reached for my phone and messaged Evie to ask if I could go over to hers. Stuff was still a bit weird between us, but that didn't change the fact that she was the only person I wanted to talk to right now.

Sorry, she replied. **It's my mum's birthday, remember? We're going out for the day**

Tomorrow then?

I'm going to Cleo's

I sat up. Hanging out at school was one thing, but going to her house was quite another.

What for??

I've got to finish my history project with Cleo.

All day?

It's a big project

Fresh tears formed in my eyes. All I wanted was my best friend and Cleo Bayford was getting in the way. Again!

I tossed my phone on my bedside table and buried my face in my pillow.

I was still lying like that when Mum knocked on my door about ten minutes later to ask if I'd 'cooled down yet'.

'Go away,' I growled, my voice all muffled.

Mum came in anyway. My pillow was
wet and snotty from where I'd been
crying. I turned it over and
rolled over to face the wall so
I wouldn't have to look at her.

'Lola,' she said.

I ignored her, hoping she'd get
the message and go away. She didn't though,
plonking herself down on the bed instead.

'Lola, I'm sorry,' she said. 'I should have given
you more of a heads-up.'

Or a heads-up at all, I thought angrily.

'Listen,' Mum said, placing her hand on my
shoulder. 'I know seeing the sold sign must have
come as a shock, but it's not like this hasn't
been on the cards for a while now. This was
always going to happen, sweetheart.'

There was a long pause.

'At least talk to me,' she added.

I stayed perfectly still, like a statue, until she
went away.

I spent the rest of the day cooped up in my
room, only coming out for meals, and leaving

the table the second I'd finished eating. Mum must have been feeling guilty because she didn't badger me to help with the washing up or have a go at me for leaving half my broccoli the way she normally does.

Sunday was just as miserable. I had a ton of homework, but I couldn't concentrate on any of it. Every few minutes my mind would wander, and I'd get mad at Mum all over again, and if I wasn't getting mad with Mum, I was torturing myself by picturing Evie at Cleo's house. I wondered what they were doing and if they were having fun. I hoped they weren't. I hoped Cleo's house was even more boring than one of Mr Grimshaw's physics lessons. I hoped that right this second, Evie was sitting there wishing she were with me instead of stupid Cleo 'Big Head' Bayford.

No such luck. On Monday morning, walking to school, when I asked Evie about her day, her entire face lit up like a Christmas tree.

'It was great!' she gushed. 'Cleo's house is huge! She's even got a hot tub!'

'What? I thought you went over there to work on your history project?'

'I did. We went in the hot tub after we'd finished, as a reward. It was *so* nice! Cleo's mum even made us the mocktails! Look!'

She dug out her phone and showed me a photo of her and Cleo in the water, sipping  bright pink drinks with curly straws and little paper umbrellas in them. They were sitting really close together, their heads touching. Just looking at them, the knot I'd had in my stomach ever since I found out they'd be spending the day together, got even tighter, squeezing at my insides.

'How was your weekend?' Evie asked.

'Fine,' I said. 'Boring.'

I watched her as she continued to scroll through pictures on her phone.

It was strange; on Saturday, I'd been *so* desperate to talk to her, but now that she was right in front of me, I found myself clamming up.

What if she took Mum's side, the same way she took Cleo's the other day? I wasn't sure I could take it if she did.

In registration, Daniel was being really annoying. He kept nudging my knee under the table then pretending to act all surprised when I told him to stop. I was glad when Mr Grimshaw sent us to the main hall for an assembly. When we arrived, I looked for Evie, but her class hadn't arrived yet, so I sat with the Alices instead.

When everyone had sat down, Mr Da Souza got up on stage and announced that on the last day of school before the half term, there would be a Year Seven and Eight Halloween disco, with prizes on offer for the best costumes.

This cheered me up a bit. I love dressing up for Halloween. Every year Evie and I go all out with our costumes, planning them weeks in advance. Last year we were Frankenstein's monster and bride. The wallpaper on my phone was a photo of the two of us before we headed out trick or treating. My face was bright green and I wore an old suit of Matthew's and a short

175

black wig Mum ordered online, and I had this
fake bolt through my neck that looks
super realistic. Next to me, Evie was
wearing a long white dress
and white face make-up and
had her black hair teased into
a beehive with two fat white
streaks.

That's when I realised
exactly what I had to do to
make sure everyone knew that
Evie was *my* best friend and
not Cleo's – I needed to come up with another
fancy dress theme for the two of us; an even
better one than last year. Once everyone saw us
together at the Halloween disco, there would be
no mistaking who was best friends with who!

My brain was buzzing for the rest of the
day. Even Daniel writing stupid little notes in
the margin of my maths book couldn't distract
me, and by lunchtime, I'd come up with a dozen
different costume ideas.

'Jack Skellington and Sally from *The
Nightmare Before Christmas*,' I said as I sat

down next to Evie, as far away from Cleo as possible.

'What on earth are you talking about?' Cleo asked.

'Halloween costumes for the disco, of course. Evie, just imagine how cool it would be! I bet Grandma Finch would help us with the sewing again.'

'It sounds like a lot of work,' she said with a frown.

'OK, how about Morticia and Gomez Addams then? I could wear my suit again.'

'Aren't they a married couple?' Cleo pointed out.

'Yes,' I said. 'So?'

'Well, isn't that a bit weird? Two girls pretending to be husband and wife?'

'No,' I scoffed. 'It's not weird at all. And anyway, it's not like we haven't done it before. Last year we went trick or treating as Frankenstein's monster and bride and it was amazing.'

'You guys were still trick or treating in Year Six?' Cleo said, screwing up her face.

'Yes. Why?'

'Well, aren't you a bit old? I stopped in like Year Four or something.'

I ignored her and turned to Evie. 'We don't have to go as a couple if you really don't want to. How about we dress up as mummies? That would be pretty easy. We just need to get a load of bandages.'

'I'm not sure I like the idea of wearing bandages to a disco,' Evie said slowly. 'What if they started unravelling?'

'Zombies then?' I suggested.

'No offence, Lola,' Cleo said, before Evie even had the chance to reply. 'But these are *hardly* flattering costumes. How is Evie supposed to impress Zane if she's pretending to be half-dead?'

'Zane?' I asked. 'Who's Zane?'

'Kieran's best friend,' Cleo replied. 'Evie *lurves* him.'

'No, I don't!' Evie squealed.

'Then why have you gone bright red?'

'I just think he's kind of cute, that's all.'

'Yeah, right. You want to marry him and have his babies!'

Evie squealed some more and covered her

face with her hands. How come *I* hadn't heard
about him?

'You need to dress up as something really
cute,' Cleo said. 'A cat or an angel.'

'An angel? What's scary about an angel?
Halloween costumes are supposed to be scary!' I
said crossly.

'Oh, I'm sorry, I wasn't aware I
was having lunch with the Halloween
police,' Cleo replied.

'How are we supposed to win a
prize if you're dressed up as a stupid
angel?' I said to Evie.

'Oh, come on, no one actually takes the
costume competition seriously,' Cleo said.

'Says who?'

'Yasmin told me, of course.'

'Of course,' I said, rolling my eyes.

'I'm only trying to help, Lola,' Cleo snapped.
'Or do you want to get it totally wrong and wind
up looking like a weirdo?'

'It's Halloween,' I shot back. 'Looking like a
weirdo is the whole point.'

'OK, fine,' Cleo said, flipping her hair over her

shoulder. 'Just don't say I didn't warn you when you turn up dressed as a disgusting monster or whatever and everyone thinks you're a total freak.' She stood up. 'I'm going to get some chips. Anyone want anything?'

'No, thanks,' Evie said.

I just looked away.

'Can you believe her?' I hissed, as soon as Cleo was out of earshot. 'As if we're going to dress up as cats or angels!'

'What's so terrible about dressing up as a cat?' Evie asked.

'Everything!' I cried.

'But it's a disco. I want to look nice.'

'Is this about that boy?' I demanded.

Evie's pink cheeks told me all I needed to know.

'How did you even meet him?'

'Cleo and I sometimes watch him playing football during morning break.'

'How do you even know that you like him then? He might have a horrible personality, or really bad breath, or not like cats!'

'See, this is the other reason why I didn't tell you,' Evie said huffily. 'Because I knew you wouldn't understand.'

'Yeah, because it makes *no* sense.'

'To you maybe.'

There was a pause.

'Are you actually serious about dressing up as an angel?' I asked sulkily. I couldn't imagine anything duller.

'God, I don't know, Lola,' Evie said. 'Maybe.' She sounded fed-up, which didn't exactly seem fair seeing as she was the one who was being annoying.

'Then what would *I* go as?' I asked.

She sighed. 'Whatever you want, Lola.'

'But then we won't be coordinating.'

'Do we always have to coordinate?'

'Of course we do!' I yelped. 'It's Halloween! We always do!' I stood up and grabbed my bag.

'Where are you going?' Evie asked.

'The library,' I said, swallowing. 'I have some homework I forgot about.'

At home time I waited at the gates for Evie like normal. After ten minutes she still hadn't

181

appeared. I messaged to see where she was.

Having dinner at Cleo's, she replied.

Why didn't you tell me?

I'm pretty sure I did

Well I'm pretty sure you didn't

I stared at my phone, waiting for a reply, but the screen remained blank, and was still blank when I got home.

Chapter Nineteen

At Wednesday's Scribble Society, we were working in pairs to plot out ghost stories. Mrs Suleman went around the room carrying a hat containing loads of slips of paper with unlikely settings written on them (places like 'Zumba class' and 'a nail bar') and asked us to pick one out.

Astrid and I pulled out 'Disneyland' and had already filled several pages with notes about a haunted runaway train.

'What are you dressing up as for the disco?' Astrid asked.

I hesitated. Evie and I hadn't spoken about costumes since Monday lunchtime. In fact, we hadn't really spoken about very much at all. We'd walked to school every day in an awkward silence, only grunting a few words at each other.

'We haven't decided yet,' I said. 'How about you?'

Astrid whipped a piece of paper out of her folder and pushed it across the table towards me.

In pencil crayon, she'd drawn a picture of a girl (who looked a whole lot like Astrid) wearing a forest green belted tunic with massive furry shoulder pads, a pair of knee-high boots and a long flowing cloak.

'Is that Cahearah?' I asked. 'From your book?'

'Bingo!' Astrid said, looking pleased that I'd remembered.

'It's amazing.'

'Thanks! The tunic is almost done. I just need to add the shoulder pads now. The material for the cloak is being delivered so I'm going to sew that next week.'

'Wait, you're making this? All by yourself?'

'Uh-huh! I've been sewing my own clothes and stuff since I was tiny.'

I was seriously impressed.

I took a closer look at the drawing.

'Is that her chakram?' I asked, pointing at the disc in Cahearah's left hand.

'Yes!' Astrid said happily. 'I'm going to spray paint my brother's Frisbee this weekend. Hey, do you want to come over? I'm going to have a Tim Burton marathon – *Beetlejuice*, *Corpse Bride* and *Edward Scissorhands*.'

'I'm sorry, but I can't,' I said. 'Evie and I are figuring out *our* Halloween costumes this Saturday.'

At least that was the plan I'd made in my head. I hadn't run it by Evie yet.

'Oh, that's too bad,' Astrid said, looking a bit disappointed. 'Another time maybe?'

'Sure.'

There was a pause.

'Listen, I'm sorry if I upset you last week,' Astrid said, doodling in the corner of her drawing.

'What are you talking about?'

'That thing I said . . . about Evie and Cleo being best friends.'

'Oh . . .' I said, blood rushing to my cheeks.

'I didn't mean to upset you. I just . . .'

Her voice trailed off.

185

'What?' I asked.

She took a deep breath.

'Don't take this the wrong way or anything, but you and Evie seem really different.'

I frowned. Evie and I weren't different. We were two peas in a pod! I had the bracelet to prove it!

Even so, I couldn't help but ask, 'Different how?'

'I guess I can't imagine Evie being interested in this,' Astrid said, pointing at her drawing.

'No, no, she would,' I insisted. 'It's Cleo who's the problem. When Evie's with me, she's a totally different person.'

'She is?' Astrid said, looking skeptical.

'One hundred per cent. Just wait until the disco – you'll see exactly what I mean.'

On Friday morning, I plucked up the courage to ask Evie if she wanted to go shopping for Halloween costumes on Saturday.

'It's probably too late for us to make anything from scratch,' I said. 'But there's definitely still time for us to buy something.'

'Do you promise you won't be all weird and stressy about it?' Evie asked.

I frowned. I wasn't the one being weird – Evie was! But I didn't want to have another argument, so I sucked it up, obediently swiping my finger across my heart.

'Promise,' I said.

Mum and I still weren't really talking, so I was glad we were spending the weekend at Dad's.

For dinner, we ordered pizza and for the first time in absolutely ages, Matthew agreed to join Dad and I for a film.

'Anything as long as it isn't *The Parent Trap*,' he said.

We ended up watching a fantasy film called *Stardust*, which everyone seemed to like. Best of all, Dad's phone didn't buzz the entire time.

'See,' I hissed at Matthew afterwards. 'I told you he doesn't have a girlfriend.'

The following morning, Dad dropped Matthew off at Samir's where he was staying the night, and me off at Evie's. After our trip into town, we were going back to hers and I was sleeping over. It felt like forever since we'd properly hung out, and although things had been a bit funny between us recently, I was excited about getting to spend some quality time with her, with no Cleo butting her nose in and ruining everything.

I dumped my overnight bag in Evie's bedroom and sat on the bed while she did her hair and applied make-up.

'How much longer are you going to be?' I asked, checking the time on my phone. 'Five Guys will be rammed if we don't get there soon.'

'Hang on,' Evie replied. 'I just need to make sure my eyes match.'

What felt like about five hours later, she spun around in her wheelie chair.

'How do I look?' she asked, crossing one leg over the other and fluttering her eyelashes.

'Like you've been punched in the face,' I replied.

Evie tutted. 'It's *called* a smoky eye,' she said. 'Cleo showed me how.'

'When?'

'When I was round at hers the other day. She's *so* good at make-up. She can even do winged eyeliner.'

'Big deal,' I muttered, pulling at a loose thread hanging from the hem of my sweatshirt.

'It is actually,' Evie snapped, turning back to admire her reflection. 'Do you have any idea how hard it is to get right?'

I rolled my eyes, not realising Evie would be able to see me in the mirror.

She spun back around in her chair.

'I know you don't like Cleo, Lola,' she said. 'But has it ever crossed your mind that I do?'

I considered this for a moment.

'But why?' I asked.

Evie frowned. 'Why do I like her?'

'Yeah.'

'Because she's nice and she's fun and she listens to me and supports me.'

'But don't I do all that stuff too?'

Evie sighed. 'People are allowed more than one friend, Lola.'

But what about best friends? I was too afraid to ask.

Five Guys was heaving by the time Evie's dad finally dropped us off in town.

'See,' I said. 'I told you we should have left earlier.'

'Oh, relax,' Evie replied, looking at something on her phone. 'We've got plenty of time.'

While we waited for our burgers to be prepared, I assumed we'd mix our very own soft drink flavour combos the way we usually did, but Evie was being really boring and just wanted a Diet Coke.

'Suit yourself,' I said, mixing together orange Fanta, cherry vanilla Coke and Dr Pepper.

We got our food and headed upstairs to find seats.

'OK,' I said as we sat down at a table in the corner. 'Would you rather eat a stranger's toenail clippings once a week *or* have everything smell like rotten eggs.'

'Lola, I'm trying to eat,' Evie said, unwrapping her burger.

'So? You know the rules. You *have* to answer.'

'Well maybe I don't want to, today.'

'Sorry, you don't have a choice . . . unless it's between toenails or rotten eggs!' I cracked up laughing.

Evie didn't join in, instead fixing me with a glare. She looked so stern that for ages I assumed she was joking.

'Oh, come on,' I said, when it dawned on me that she was actually being serious. 'Don't be boring. Just answer it.'

I began to wiggle my fingers.

'I said I don't want to,' Evie snapped, pushing my hand away.

'OK, OK,' I said, holding up my hands in surrender. 'There's no need to bite my head off. I was just trying to have a bit of fun.'

 'Well, I'm not in the mood right now.'

'Clearly,' I muttered, rolling my eyes as I bit into my burger.

We ate our food quickly then headed over to Abracadabra, the big fancy dress shop on the high street. As we walked, Evie looked at her phone while I thought about what had just happened. Evie and I had been grossing each other out with *Would You Rather?* questions for years – that was literally the entire point of the game! Since when did she change the rules without telling me? I wanted to ask her, but at the same time, I didn't want to turn it into a big thing, so I kept my mouth shut and decided to concentrate on getting our costumes sorted instead.

'Are you sure you don't want to go as Morticia and Gomez?' I asked as we made our way down the central aisle in Abracadabra.

'Positive,' Evie said.

I frowned. 'Then who?'

'How about the three witches from *Hocus Pocus*?'

'But there's only two of us.'

'I know that, silly! Cleo can be the third.'

'Cleo? No way!'

'Why not?'

'Because I'd rather eat a stranger's toenail clippings *and* smell like rotten eggs.'

Evie looked at me. 'Well, that's really mature, Lola.'

'I'm just being honest.'

'No, you're just acting like a brat because you're not getting your own way.'

My eyes almost popped out of my head. 'Me?' I cried. 'I'm not the one who has rejected every single costume idea I've suggested.'

'Yes, because they're all weird. And you've rejected everything I've suggested too, remember?'

'Only because they're all so *boring*.'

'To you maybe.'

'Oh, come on, Evie, a cat is about as boring as it gets!'

'What are you talking about? You love cats!'

'That doesn't mean I want to dress up as one!'

'Well, I'd rather look "boring" than like a total freak.'

'Did Cleo tell you to say that?'

Evie's nostrils flared the way they only ever do when she's really cross. 'I can think for myself, you know.'

'Oh yeah?'

'Yeah!'

'Well, you could have fooled me.'

Just then, Evie's phone buzzed. She read what was on the screen and let out an excited little yelp.

'Who is it?' I asked, grabbing a pointy witch's hat from the shelf and putting it on. It was too big for me, falling over my eyes.

'It's Cleo,' Evie said. 'She's asking us if we want to meet her at the cinema.'

Oh great. 'When?' I asked.

'Now.'

I whipped off the hat. 'But we're busy.'

'She's with Kieran and Zane.'

'So?'

Evie grabbed hold of my arms. 'Lola, this is my chance to talk to him! Properly!'

'But we still haven't figured out our costumes!'

Evie tutted, like it wasn't even important. 'We can come back afterwards,' she said. 'Please, Lola!' She pressed her hands together

194

in prayer position and fluttered her eyelashes.

'But this is meant to be *our* day!' I cried.

'I'll make it up to you.'

'How?'

She looked around her frantically.

'I . . . I . . . I'll wear any Halloween costume you choose.'

'Any?'

'Yes.'

'You promise?'

'Yes.'

'On Twiglet's life.'

'On Twiglet's life, I swear.'

I stared at her face, aglow with excitement. For the first time all day, she looked like the Evie I knew and loved.

'OK, fine,' I said.

She let out a squeal and threw her arms around me.

'Thank you!' she cried. 'You won't regret this, Lola, I'm telling you!'

But as she dragged me out of the shop, I already felt unsure.

Chapter Twenty

Evie's mood was transformed as we walked to the cinema. She even linked her arms with me, for the first time in what seemed like ages.

'Over here!' Cleo called as we walked into the foyer.

I'd never seen her out of school uniform before. She looked at least fourteen in high-heeled leather boots and an expensive looking cream coat. She was standing in the queue for tickets with two boys.

'Which one is Zane?' I asked Evie as we made our way towards them.

'Shush!' she hissed. 'He might hear you!'

Cleo introduced us all.

'You've already met the lovely Evie,' she said, presenting Evie like she was first prize in a game show. 'And this is her friend, Lola. Lola, this is

my boyfriend Kieran and
his best friend Zane.'

With his pouty lips and
floppy hair, Zane looked
like a proper poser. I bet
his camera roll was full of selfies.

'She your little sister or something?' he asked,
nodding at me.

Cleo let out a peal of laughter.

'Oh, Zane, don't be so silly,' she said, hitting
him on the arm. 'She's in our year.'

'You're joking?'

'Of course not. Why else would we let her
hang around with us? She's a late bloomer,' Cleo
said. 'Right, Lola?'

'Right,' I muttered as the boys
sniggered and repeated 'late
bloomer' under their breath like
it was the punchline to a joke.

I glanced at Evie, who was
staring up at Zane in wonder. I
couldn't believe *this* was the boy
she liked. He was a total idiot!

I looked at the film listings above the counter

and realised that I had no idea which film we were supposed to be watching.

'What are we even seeing?' I asked.

'*Fatal Flaw 2: Overkill,*' Kieran replied. 'It looks sick!'

Kieran was tall and blond and reeked of aftershave.

'You saw the first one, right?' Zane asked Evie.

'Of course,' she said, nodding enthusiastically. 'I loved it.'

I stared at her in disbelief. What on earth was she talking about? Evie can't *stand* action films.

Before I had the chance to point this out, it was our turn to be served.

Cleo took charge.

'Five for *Fatal Flaw 2,*' she said.

The guy behind the counter looked at us all in turn, but stopped when he got to me.

'How old are you?' he asked.

'Twelve,' I replied.

'Got any ID?'

'No. Why?'

'*Fatal Flaw 2* is a 12A. If you're under

twelve, you can't watch it without an adult accompanying you.'

'But I'm not under twelve,' I said, standing up as straight as I could. 'I was twelve in September.'

'That's fine,' the guy behind the counter said. 'I just need to see some ID to support that.'

'But I don't have any.'

'In that case, I'm sorry,' he said, not looking sorry at all, 'but I can't sell you a ticket without seeing some proof of age. We could lose our licence if we were found to be admitting under-twelves without an adult.'

'But I'm not *under* twelve!' I protested. 'I *am* twelve!'

'She's telling the truth,' Cleo said. 'It's not *her* fault she looks so young for her age.'

The guy behind the counter shrugged. 'Like I said, I'm sorry, but there's nothing I can do.'

'What about the rest of us?' Zane asked. 'We can still see it, right?'

'Yeah, no problem.'

'Phew!'

'But that's not fair!' I cried. Of the five of us, only three were actually twelve, and *I* was one of them!

'The new Pixar is due to start in about ten minutes,' the guy said. 'That's a PG.'

'Can't she just watch that instead?' Kieran asked.

Cleo's face lit up. 'That's actually a really good idea,' she said, turning to me. 'That's OK with you, right, Lola? We can all meet up in the foyer afterwards.'

I looked to Evie; sure she'd say no, that this was the complete opposite of a 'really good idea'.

But Evie turned to me a bit guiltily and said, 'Would you mind watching that one?'

'I'm going to have to hurry you,' the guy behind the counter said. 'There are people waiting.'

'I need to speak to you,' I said to Evie, my heart hammering in my chest.

I marched over to the pick and mix, leaving her to scamper after me. I came to a stop next to the cola bottles and jelly beans.

'Are you serious?' I hissed.

'I might never get a chance like this again!'

'A chance to do what? Watch some stupid action film you wouldn't ordinarily be interested in in a billion years?'

'I'm talking about getting a chance to spend some time with Zane,' she said, peeking over her shoulder.

'Him?' I cried. 'The boy who just made fun of me to my face?'

'He was just messing around. I really don't think he meant it like that.'

I was vibrating with anger.

'Fine,' I said, folding my arms and angling my body away from her so she wouldn't see the tears welling up in my eyes. 'Do what you want.'

'Oh, please don't be like this, Lola.'

'How do you expect me to be?' I cried.

'I don't know. Excited for me?'

I snorted. *As if!*

'Are you ready, Evie?' Cleo asked, appearing at Evie's side holding a massive carton of popcorn. 'The film's starting any minute.'

When Evie hesitated, Cleo turned to me, a disapproving expression on her face.

'I really hope you're not trying to bully her into skipping the film, Lola,' she said sternly.

'This has nothing to do with you,' I snapped.

She raised an eyebrow.

'Well, I'm sorry, but Evie's my friend and I'm here to support her.'

'She doesn't *need* your support. She's already got me; her *best* friend.'

'Some best friend!'

'What's that supposed to mean?' I asked, fresh anger whipping up like a tornado in my belly.

'A *true* best friend would realise how important this is to Evie. A *true* best friend would be happy for her, not make a big fuss and go storming off in a sulk.'

'How would you know?' I cried. 'Your best friend was so keen to get away from you, she moved all the way to Australia!'

'Excuse me?' Cleo said, flushing.

'You heard me!'

'Stop it!' Evie cried. 'Both of you!'

'She started it!' I yelled, jabbing my index finger towards Cleo.

'No, Lola,' Cleo said, staring at me. '*You* started it. *You're* the one who's jealous. And *you're* the one who hates the fact that Evie prefers hanging out with me.'

'That's not true!'

'Yes, it is! Then why did Evie tell me just the other day that she feels way closer to me these days than she does to you?'

I felt like that time I jumped off a swing in the park and winded myself; like all the breath had been sucked out of my body.

'You're lying,' I said, my voice wobbling all over the place.

I turned to Evie.

'She's lying, isn't she?'

Evie's eyes filled with tears.

'Stop getting at her,' Cleo snapped, putting a protective arm around Evie's shoulder. 'Can't you see that she's upset? No wonder your parents called you Lola. *Lady of Sorrows* is the perfect name for you.' She pulled Evie closer to her.

Hatred surged through my body.

How dare she?

HOW DARE SHE?

'This is all your fault, Cleo Bayford!' I roared.
'Me and Evie were fine before you came along.
You're the one who ruined everything, nobody
else – you!'

I balled my hand into a fist and
punched her carton of popcorn
as hard as I could. The entire
thing went up in the air, kernels
raining down on us like confetti.

People were staring and my
heart was beating so fast I
thought it might leap out of my chest.

'Oh. My. God,' Cleo said, picking a piece
of popcorn off her coat and popping it in her
mouth. 'Lola Kite, you are out of control. No
wonder you get on so well with witchy Astrid
Chaney. You're like two peas in a pod!'

I looked at Evie, desperate for her to take my
side and admit that Cleo had been lying after all,
that *she* was the one in the wrong, not me, but

she didn't say a word. She wouldn't even look at me, her hands covering her mouth and nose, her eyes staring down at the popcorn-covered carpet.

Fresh tears welling in my eyes, I tried to undo the clasp of my peas-in-a-pod bracelet, but my fingers were trembling too much. I hooked them underneath the chain instead and pulled as hard as I could, snapping it.

'There!' I cried, flinging it at Cleo's feet. 'If you're such *wonderful* friends, you can have it!'

Then I turned and ran towards the exit before they could see me cry.

Chapter Twenty-One

I ran all the way back to Dad's, hot tears streaming down my face. A lady tried to stop me and check I was OK, but I yelled at her to leave me alone and kept on running, terrified that if I stopped, I'd crumple like a house of cards.

At Dad's building, someone was leaving so I was able to slip inside without having to buzz up.

In the lift, I caught sight of my reflection in

 the mirrored panel. I looked awful – all puffy and blotchy, the way I get in summer when I have hay fever. I wiped my face with my sleeve and hoped Dad wouldn't notice. I'd

tell him that there'd been a change of plan and that I wasn't staying over at Evie's after all. He probably wouldn't think to call Evie's house to check my story the way Mum would.

At the eighth floor, I got out and hurried down the corridor to Dad's flat.

I paused outside the door and took a deep breath before pressing the doorbell. Inside, I could hear music playing and Dad moving around. I couldn't wait to see him – maybe we could order pizza, watch a film, eat some ice cream, pretend this afternoon never happened, at least for a few hours.

The door swung open but instead of Dad on the other side, it was a woman I'd never seen before – a woman with short blonde hair and glasses, wearing Dad's ancient University of York hoodie and a pair of his woolly walking socks.

'Who are you?' I blurted out.

'Hello,' the woman said, smiling at me. 'I'm Kirsty.'

Kirsty.

Matthew had been right all along.

I backed away from the door, my heart thumping.

'Are you Lola?' she asked. 'Hang on, I'll just get your dad.' She turned away from the door. 'Glenn!' she called. 'Glenn!'

But I didn't hang on.

I turned and ran back down the corridor as fast as my legs could carry me and I ran and ran and ran.

I ran until I got a stitch and had to stop. Looking around me, I realised I had no idea where I was. The street I was on was quiet, just a row of scruffy houses with banged-up front doors and dingy blinds hanging in the windows. I pulled out my phone to try to figure out where I'd ended up. Dad must have called Mum because I had a load of missed calls and messages from both of them on my phone.

As I started to scroll through them, Mum called. This time, I answered.

'Lola!' she cried. 'Where are you?'

She sounded really worried.

'I don't know,' I said, starting to cry.

'Send me a drop pin,' she said briskly. 'I'm coming to get you.'

Mum only took fifteen minutes to get to me, but it felt like longer. I sat on the curb and stared at my trainers. They were the rainbow ones I got for my birthday. They were already a bit dirty.

I was still staring at them when Mum pulled up.

She wound down the window and gestured for me to get in the car. 'Are you OK, Lola?'

I opened my mouth to answer her, but no words came out. I started to cry and very quickly realised I couldn't stop.

'Oh, Lola, oh, darling,' Mum said, reaching over to hug me. 'Come here.'

I let her hold me and stroke my hair as I sobbed and snotted on her sweatshirt.

'Here,' she said, once I'd calmed down a bit, leaning across me to open the glove box. 'Have a tissue.'

I took one out of the packet and wiped my

face and blew my nose. 'Everything is awful,'
I said, my voice all jerky. 'Evie hates me, and
you've sold the house, and Dad has a secret . . .'

I stopped talking.

'A secret what?' Mum asked gently.

I shook my head. 'Nothing.'

Mum reached for my hand.

'Lola, I know about Kirsty,' she
said.

My head snapped up. 'You do? How?'

'Your dad told me.'

'When?'

'When he started seeing her. About a month
ago, I think.'

I was stunned. Mum had known this entire
time?

'And you don't mind?' I asked.

'Of course not. And even if I did, your dad's
a grown-up. It's nothing to do with me, not any
more.'

'But if dad has a girlfriend, how are you
supposed to get back together?'

Mum frowned. 'Get back together?' she
repeated.

I nodded.

'I thought you might realise how much you miss each other, and get back together, and things could go back to how they were before.'

'Oh, sweetheart,' Mum said.

I looked down at my lap and blinked hard, determined not to start crying again.

Mum pulled on her seatbelt.

'I think it might be a good time for you, me and your dad to have a chat,' she said, starting the engine.

Fifteen minutes later we were in Dad's flat. I sat in the living room while Mum and Dad made tea in the kitchen and spoke to one another in low voices. Kirsty was nowhere to be seen.

Mum and Dad came in, carrying their drinks on a tray, and sat down on the sofa. I stayed where I was, in the armchair, curled up in a ball.

Mum spoke first.

'Lola, we need you to know that your dad and I are not going to get back together, but that's got nothing to do with Kirsty, OK?'

I didn't say anything.

Mum leaned forward.

'We didn't get a divorce on a whim, darling,' she said. 'It was a big decision, and we didn't take it lightly.'

'But it was *your* decision,' I said. 'You were the one who wanted to get divorced. If you hadn't, you'd still be married, and Dad would still be living with us, and we wouldn't have to sell the house.'

Mum and Dad exchanged looks. Dad cleared his throat.

'Your mum was the one who initiated the break-up, Lola, yes, but only because I wasn't brave enough to do it myself. The moment she suggested it, I knew that it was the right thing to do.'

'Then why did you cry like that? If it was "right", why were you so upset?'

'I'm sorry, sweetheart, I don't know what you're talking about,' Dad said, looking confused.

'The night before you moved out. You came into my bedroom and cried for ages and ages.'

Mum turned to look at him.

'Ah,' Dad said, his cheeks turning pink. 'I thought you were asleep.'

I shook my head.

'I'm sorry, sweetheart, that can't have been nice to hear. But, you see, I was crying because I was sad, because it was a sad situation. But that doesn't mean the divorce was a mistake, or that your mum is to blame in any way. Things were tough at first, for both of us, in lots of different ways, but we're in firm agreement now that we're so much happier apart than together.'

'But what about me? *I'm* not happier.'

Mum and Dad's faces fell like dominoes.

'Oh, sweetheart,' Mum said, getting up and squeezing next to me on the armchair. 'I know the split hit you hard, and honestly, seeing you upset is the worst thing about all of this. But you'll understand when you're older, I promise.'

I was so sick of being told that I'd understand when I was older. Even if it turned out to be true, it didn't help me *now*.

213

'Why does everything have to change?' I asked, a fresh tear trickling down my cheek.

As the words left my mouth, I realised I wasn't talking about Mum and Dad, or Kirsty, or moving house.

I was talking about Evie.

For such a long time, our friendship was the one thing in my life that always stayed the same, and now I didn't even have that. I started to cry again.

'Because . . . that's life,' Dad said. 'And not all change is bad, Lola, I promise. Sometimes change is fun and exciting. And sometimes it takes a bit longer to get used to, but that doesn't mean it's always going to feel painful, I promise you.'

What he was saying sort of made sense, but being told that I was going to feel rubbish for a long time before I felt better wasn't exactly the news I wanted to hear.

Mum leaned over and wiped my tears away with her thumbs.

'Now, what's all this nonsense about Evie hating you?' she asked.

'It's not nonsense, it's true.'

'Oh, I doubt that. You two have been best friends forever.'

'Not any more,' I said fiercely.

'But what on earth happened?' Dad wanted to know.

I buried my face in my knees.

'I don't want to talk about it.'

It was too awful, too embarrassing, too painful.

'But how can we help if you won't talk to us?' Mum asked.

'That's just it, you can't,' I said in a muffled voice.

'You could try us?'

I shook my head hard.

There was no point. Evie had already picked Cleo over me, and it hurt more than I could ever have imagined.

Chapter Twenty-Two

The next day, I felt really sad and empty.

When I got back from Dad's on Sunday evening, I went straight up to my bedroom. The first thing I saw was my fortune waving cat sitting innocently on the windowsill. I picked it up.

'Some good luck charm you are,' I said, opening my old toy cupboard and flinging it right to the very back.

I paced up and down, nervous energy dancing through my arms and legs, feeling like my whole body was about to erupt. I turned around and spotted a notepad on my desk. Lunging for it, I turned to a clean page. Then I started to write, just like we did at the beginning of each Scribble Society session, only this time there was no Mrs Suleman telling us when to stop. So I didn't. I just kept going, filling page after page, only putting down my pen when Mum knocked on the door about half an hour later to check if I was OK.

I wasn't, but I definitely felt a little bit less awful, and that was better than nothing.

On Monday, when Mum came into my room to wake me up for school, I rolled onto my side clutching my belly and told her I wasn't feeling well. I could tell she knew I was lying, but she must have felt sorry for me, because after touching my forehead with the back of her hand, she told me I could have the day off.

'I'll call Evie's mum and let her know you won't be calling for her this morning,' she said.

'Don't bother,' I muttered.

Mum paused in the doorway.

'Are you sure you don't want to tell me what happened between the two of you?' she asked.

'Positive,' I replied, pulling the duvet over my head.

I spent most of the day torturing myself by picturing Evie and Cleo at school together. I bet Cleo was saying loads of mean things about me. The thought that Evie probably agreed with them made me want to never come out from under my duvet ever again.

On Tuesday, I told Mum I was still feeling poorly.

'Please,' I begged, when she folded her arms and looked skeptical. 'Just one more day.'

She sighed.

'OK,' she said. 'But you're going back tomorrow, no arguments.'

I tried my luck again on Wednesday, but this time Mum was having none of it.

'Come on,' she said, pulling the duvet off me. 'I'll give you a lift.'

When I arrived at school, I went straight to registration so I wouldn't bump into Evie or Cleo.

Daniel was already there. When he saw me, his face lit up, which was all I needed.

'Tinkerbell!' he cried, opening his arms. 'I missed you!'

I ignored him and dumped my backpack on the desk.

'Hey, do you want to hear a joke?' he asked.

'No.'

'Aw, don't be like that.'

'I'll be however I want to be,' I growled. 'Now leave me alone.'

'But it's a really good one!'

I ignored him.

He didn't get the message. 'What do you call a spider with seven legs?' he began.

'I said, I don't want to hear it!' I roared, shoving him off his chair as hard as I could.

He went flying, landing on the floor with a thump.

'What on earth is going on?' Mr Grimshaw bellowed as he strode into the room. 'Why is Daniel on the

floor?' he demanded, looking at me accusingly.

My heart plummeted; that was all I needed – a bunch of conduct marks to make my already terrible day even worse.

'I fell, sir,' Daniel said.

I blinked in surprise.

'You fell?' Mr Grimshaw said, frowning.

'Yes, sir. It was nothing to do with Lola, honest.'

Mr Grimshaw looked from Daniel to me, then back to Daniel again, his frown deepening. I could tell he didn't believe him.

'Well, get up then,' he said eventually.

Daniel scrambled to his feet and sat down next to me.

Neither of us said a word for the rest of tutor time.

At lunch, I didn't go to the canteen. Instead, I went round the back of the tennis courts and ate the bag of crisps and the chocolate bar I'd bought from the tuck shop during morning break.

After school, I skipped Scribble Society. I didn't want to risk running into Evie and Cleo in the corridor afterwards. I'd managed to get through the whole day without seeing either of them and I was determined to keep it that way for as long as I could.

On Thursday, I caught a glimpse of Evie and Cleo at morning break. They were huddled on a bench in the courtyard sharing a packet of crisps and giggling.

No one seemed to notice we weren't talking. Why would they? If Astrid was anything to go by, most of the people at Henry Bigg Academy thought *Cleo* was Evie's best friend.

This wasn't the first time Evie and I had fallen out, but it had always been over silly stuff before, and we'd always made up in a matter of hours.

This time felt different.

This time felt final.

Chapter Twenty-Three

On Friday all anyone could talk about was the
disco – what they were going to wear and which
songs they were going to ask the DJ to play.
This time last week, I'd been so excited about
going, but now all I wanted to do was crawl in
a hole and not come out until it was all over.
Maybe Evie was going to dress up with Cleo
now instead. The thought of them in matching
costumes made me want to throw up.

That morning, I'd persuaded Mum to write me
a note so I could get out of PE. If I was sitting
on the bench, at least I could keep out of Evie
and Cleo's way. But luckily the entire group was
sent on a cross-country run around the school
grounds, and I didn't have to see them at all.

I went to wait in the PE department office. When
I walked in, I saw Astrid sitting on the bench.

'I nearly chopped my finger off cutting out the shield for my Cahearah costume,' she said cheerfully, holding up a bandaged hand. 'Luckily, there's a sequence in my novel where Cahearah almost slices off *her* finger when her arch nemesis enchants her chakram, so it's *totally* in character.'

'Cool,' I murmured, sitting next to her but not really paying attention.

'Did you and Evie decide what you're dressing up as in the end?' she asked.

'Oh. No,' I said, blood rushing to my cheeks.

'You didn't? How come?'

'I'm not going to the disco.'

Astrid's face fell.

'Why?'

'It's this stomachache,' I said, rubbing my belly. 'I've had it all week.'

'Is that why you missed Scribble Society on Wednesday?'

'Uh-huh.' I felt awful lying to Astrid, but I didn't know what else to do.

'Well, it's too bad you won't be there tonight,'

she said, poking at her bandage. 'I was kind of hoping we could hang out . . .'

'Maybe some other time,' I muttered.

'Right,' Astrid said, chewing on her lower lip and looking out the window.

As soon as the bell rang, I bolted for the exit. All I wanted to do was go home, watch TV, eat junk and get this evening over and done with. At least next week was half term and I wouldn't have to see anyone.

The second I got home, I got changed out of my uniform, loaded up on snacks, and headed to the living room. I usually get the house to myself for a few hours, so I was surprised when Matthew walked through the front door about ten minutes after me. Instead of heading straight upstairs to game, like he usually did, he came into the living room.

'All right?' he said, flopping down on the sofa next to me.

I ignored him and kept watching the TV. I waited for him to go away, but he didn't.

'How come you're not getting ready for your little disco?' he asked, propping his stinky feet on the coffee table.

'Duh! Because I'm not going,' I muttered.

'Why not? Because of what happened with Evie?'

'How do you know about that?' I blurted out.

'Those pages from your diary.'

'What are you talking about? I don't keep a diary.'

'Yeah, you do. I'd recognise your terrible handwriting anywhere. Some scribbled pages were in your bin.'

'What were you doing looking in my bin?' I demanded. He must have seen my free-write from Sunday!

'Calm down! I wasn't. Mum told me to empty all the bins and it was sitting right on top. It was practically asking to be read.'

'I don't care,' I snapped. 'You weren't supposed to read it. No one was.'

'Well, I did, so it's too late now.'

'Well, it's nothing,' I said, folding my arms across my chest. 'I didn't even mean half of it.'

'So, you didn't have a total hissy fit in the cinema last weekend then?'

'None of your business.'

'I'm going to take that as a yes,' he said with a smirk.

'Well, no one asked you, did they?' I replied, turning up the volume.

'So, is that it then?' Matthew asked. 'You're just going to hide out here until the end of time?'

'No,' I lied.

'Then why aren't you going to the disco?'

'Why do you even care?'

'Because I reckon you'll regret it if you don't.'

'Yeah, well that's what *you* think.'

There was a long pause and I hoped that that would be the end of it and Matthew would leave me alone. Instead, he removed his blazer and tie like he was here to stay.

'You know,' he said, undoing the buttons on

his shirt cuffs and rolling up the sleeves, 'kind of the same thing happened to me when I was in Year Seven.'

I pretended not to hear him.

'I didn't make a massive scene and chuck popcorn everywhere,' he went on. 'But some of the other stuff that you wrote about kind of rang a bell.'

I sighed, paused the TV, and turned to face him. 'Number one, I didn't *throw* popcorn everywhere, I knocked the carton out of Cleo's hand, and number two, what are you *even* talking about?'

'Do you remember Cameron?'

'Of course I do.'

Matthew and Cameron were mates all through primary school. They always used to gang up on me and Evie and try to gross us out. One time they almost tricked us into drinking milkshakes with chopped up dead worms in them. They got into *so* much trouble when Mum found out.

'When we moved up to Henry Bigg, Cameron

joined the football team and stopped hanging around with me,' Matthew said. 'We didn't have a big falling out or anything, he just stopped calling for me, and talking to me, and stuff. Then in Year Eight, I got chatting to Samir about gaming and now *he's* my best mate.'

'And your point is?'

Matthew sighed.

'My *point*, Lola, is that hardly anyone I know is best friends now with the person they were best friends with when they were a little kid.'

'And?'

'It's totally normal!'

'Me and Evie are different.'

'That's not what your diary says.'

'It's not a diary!' I cried.

'Well, whatever it is, you shouldn't let the fact that you and Evie have fallen out stop you from going to the disco.'

 I didn't say anything. Just the thought of walking into the disco on my own and seeing Evie and Cleo there together made me feel hot all over.

'Listen,' Matthew said. 'If me and Cam

hadn't drifted apart, I might not have got to know Samir, which would have been really rubbish, because, you know, Samir is the best.'

I peered up at him. I'd never heard him talk about Samir like that before. They usually just grunt and call one another stupid nicknames.

'I'm not saying you and Evie won't work things out,' Matthew continued. 'I mean, maybe you will, I don't know. But if you don't, it's probably not the end of the world.'

'Then why does it feel that way?' I asked in a small voice.

He shrugged. 'Because stuff ending is sad, I guess. Just like Mum and Dad splitting up was sad. But that doesn't mean it's always going to feel that way.'

'You never seemed all that sad,' I pointed out.

Matthew frowned. 'About what?'

'Mum and Dad getting divorced. You never seemed to care all that much.'

'Just because I wasn't boo-hooing all the time, it doesn't mean I didn't care,' he said.

'Some people just deal with stuff differently.'

'So you *did* care?'

He tutted. 'Of course I did. I'm not a robot.'

'Oh.'

Until now, it hadn't really occurred to me that Matthew might have found the divorce hard too. He'd just carried on holing up in his room on his computer, the same as always.

But that's not really the point,' Matthew continued. 'What I'm trying to say is that this might feel really rubbish for a while. But until it doesn't, you can't spend the entire time hiding at home, eating crisps and watching telly; that's only going to make things feel worse.'

I thought of all my classmates dancing and having fun without me. I pictured Astrid dressed up as Cahearah and how disappointed she'd looked earlier when I told her I wasn't going. She'd never said so out loud, but I got the feeling she didn't have a whole lot of friends at Henry Bigg.

'It's too late,' I said, shaking my head. 'I don't even have a costume.'

'Then we'll make one.'

'Don't be crazy. The disco starts in less than an hour.'

Matthew stood up. 'We'd better get on with it then.'

Chapter Twenty-Four

By the time Mum got home from work, I was ready to go.

The costume was Matthew's idea. We got an old sweatshirt and glued an empty Coco Pops box to the front and an empty Cornflakes box to the back. We inserted a load of disposable wooden knives into both boxes, securing them with sticky tape, then used a red Sharpie to add blood splatters.

I'd teamed it with simple black leggings and trainers.

'What on earth are you supposed to be?' Mum asked, walking around me in a circle.

'Duh!' Matthew said. 'She's a cereal killer, of course.'

'Oh, honestly,' Mum said, laughing.

I was quiet on the drive to school, my cereal killer sweatshirt sitting on my lap so I wouldn't crush the boxes. Matthew came with us. He even let me sit in the passenger seat instead of making me go in the back like he normally did.

The closer we got, the more nervous I felt. I kept thinking about what Matthew had told me; about what happened with him and Cameron. Even though that story had a happy ending, the thought of me and Evie not being best friends forever, like we had always promised, made my insides ache.

We pulled up outside the school gates. I undid my seatbelt and with Mum's help, carefully pulled my sweatshirt on over my head.

'Knock 'em dead,' Matthew

said, pretending to strike an imaginary cymbal.

'Oh, Matty,' Mum said with a groan. 'That's dreadful!'

I gave them both a nervous smile, then, before I could chicken out, slid out of the car, and strode towards the gates.

Despite what Cleo had said, about people not really making a big effort with costumes, almost everyone was dressed up. There were witches and wizards and zombies and skeletons and Marvel superheroes and villains everywhere I looked.

I was halfway up the drive when Daniel appeared at my side.

'I thought that was you, titch,' he said.

I glared at him. Ever since our bust-up in registration the other morning, we'd been weirdly polite with each other, but I should have known it wouldn't last.

'What are you supposed to be?' he asked, looking me up and down.

'At least I'm wearing a costume,' I shot back.

Daniel was just in jeans and a hoodie. 'What are you talking about?' he said. 'I'm a Muggle!'

I rolled my eyes. But it was quite funny and I smiled.

'Seriously though,' Daniel said. 'What *are* you dressed up as?'

'Figure it out, pea brain,' I replied, striding on ahead.

As I walked through the main entrance, I heard someone call my name.

It was Alice B. She and Alice L were in the queue to get signed in. They looked amazing as two of the Ghostbusters. They'd even made their own proton packs out of cardboard boxes and vacuum cleaner attachments.

'My mum says if I lose or break any of the bits, I have to buy her a new vacuum out of my pocket money,' Alice L said.

'What have you come as, Lola?' Alice B asked.

'Guess,' I said.

'Um, someone who died in the cereal aisle?'

'Nope.'

'Someone with a fatal reaction to cereal?' Alice L suggested.

'You're getting closer.'

'Cereal killer!' they both cried in unison.

'Bingo.'

'That's so clever,' Alice L gushed as Alice B pumped her head up and down in agreement.

'Thanks,' I said (I couldn't wait to tell Matthew).

We entered the hall together. It looked pretty cool, all decked out with black and orange balloons and streamers. In front of the stage, there was a DJ booth, its lights programmed to flash Halloween colours – orange, green and purple – in time with the music.

'I love this song!' Alice B yelped. 'Come on, let's dance!'

I hesitated. The dance floor was still pretty empty.

'I'm going to get a drink first,' I said. 'I'll come find you in a bit.'

I followed the signs to the pop-up tuck shop. It was being manned by Mr Grimshaw and Mrs Suleman. Mr Grimshaw had teamed his usual brown suit with a pair of devil horns, but Mrs Suleman had gone the whole hog and had come as Elphaba from the musical *Wicked*. She'd even painted her hands green.

'Lola!' she said as I reached the front of the queue. 'I missed you this week. Lola is one of my Scribblers,' she told Mr Grimshaw proudly.

Hearing her say that made me feel really nice, and when she asked me if I planned on coming back after the half term holiday, I found myself saying 'yes' right away.

I bought a can of fizzy pop and headed back out into the corridor. I was about to take a sip when I heard a loud shriek that almost made me drop the can.

Astrid was making her way towards me, looking absolutely incredible in her Cahearah costume, her green cloak billowing out behind her as she walked.

'What are you doing here?' she asked, her eyes shining. 'I thought you weren't coming!'

'I changed my mind,' I said. 'You look amazing by the way! Like something out of a film!'

Astrid beamed and did a twirl. 'Thank you!' she said. 'I'm so happy with how it turned out. Although Mr Da Souza has already confiscated my shield *and* my chakram. He reckons they're a health and safety hazard or something.'

She took a step backwards and looked me up and down.

'You're a cereal killer,' she proclaimed after a few seconds.

'I didn't have much time for anything else,' I admitted.

'Who cares? I love it!' Astrid insisted. 'And at least you haven't come as a cat. Honestly, I've seen *so* many girls dressed as cats tonight.'

I wondered if Evie was one of them.

Astrid must have read my mind because the next thing she asked was if Evie and I had come together.

'No,' I said. 'We're, er, we're not really friends any more.'

'Oh. I'm sorry. Do you want to talk about it or anything?'

'Not right now,' I said quietly.

Astrid nodded in understanding.

'But maybe some other time? Over half term maybe?' I added.

A slow smile spread across Astrid's face; one I couldn't help but return.

'I'd like that,' she said. 'I'd like that a lot.'

In the hall, they'd just started playing 'Monster Mash'.

'What do you think? Shall we?' Astrid said, offering me her arm.

'OK,' I said, taking a deep breath and letting her lead me towards the music. As we made our way across the dance floor, I scanned the hall for Evie, but it was crowded, and I couldn't see her anywhere.

The Alices were dancing in front of the DJ booth.

'Oh my gosh, I love your costume,' Alice L said, gazing at Astrid's cloak in wonder.

'Did you hire it?' Alice B chimed in, reaching to stroke one of the fluffy shoulder pads.

'No,' Astrid said. 'I made it.'

The Alices gasped.

'All by yourself?'
Alice L asked.

'Uh-huh.'

'Could you teach us?' Alice B asked.

'Sure!' Astrid said happily. 'I'm Astrid, by the way.'

'I'm Alice,' the Alices said in unison, before dissolving into giggles.

'This is Alice L, and this is Alice B,' I said. 'They're in my tutor group. Astrid is in 7M.'

The *Ghostbusters* theme tune began to play. The Alices let out a scream of excitement and began to dance. Astrid and I pretended to be ghosts while the Alices blasted us with their proton packs. By the end of the song, our tummies were hurting from laughing so much.

For the next song, the four of us formed a circle and took it in turns to perform a ridiculous dance move that everyone else then had to copy. When it was my turn, I strutted around like a chicken – bum out, arms flapping – not caring one bit that I looked totally ridiculous.

We carried on like that for song after song, our circle gradually getting wider as more and more people joined in with the game.

And it was fun. It was *really* fun. In fact, it was easily the most fun I'd had since coming to Henry Bigg Academy.

After what felt like no time at all, the music stopped abruptly, and the costume competition was announced. Everyone who wanted to take part was told to line up next to the stage.

Astrid tried to persuade me to enter, but I told her and the Alices to go ahead without me.

While I waited for them to be judged, I felt a sharp tug on my sleeve.

Evie?

No.

It was Daniel.

'I've finally figured it out,' he said, looking pleased with himself. 'You're a cereal killer!'

'See, I *knew* you'd get there in the end.'

'I actually kind of wish I'd thought of it,' he said, giving my cereal boxes an admiring look.

'It was my brother's idea,' I admitted. 'And I'm pretty sure *he* got it off the internet.'

Daniel shrugged. 'Either way, nicely played, Lola Kite.'

I blinked.

'What's wrong?' Daniel asked, suddenly looking a bit worried. 'You're not going to attack me again, are you?'

'No, nothing like that,' I said quickly. I was just in shock. Because, for the first time in forever, Daniel Littleton had called me by my actual name.

After another half an hour of dancing, it was time for the costume competition results.

The Alices didn't win the 'best group costume' category (a bunch of boys who had come as Minions did) but they didn't seem to mind.

Astrid won the 'best homemade' category, just like I knew she would. I clapped for her so hard, my hands were sore.

'I'll get us some crisps to celebrate,' I declared

242

when she returned from the stage, clutching her shiny trophy.

I was on my way back from the tuck shop, two packets of crisps clutched in each fist, when I walked slap-bang into someone.

Evie.

For a few seconds, neither of us said anything; we just stared at each other.

Evie was dressed as an angel in a floaty white dress, wings and a halo made out of wire and silver tinsel. The longer we stared at one another, the pinker her cheeks became, her mouth hovering open like she wanted to say something but couldn't decide on the words.

'Cool costume,' she said finally.

She seemed really nervous, fiddling with the straps for her wings.

'Thanks,' I said, looking down at my cereal boxes. 'Yours too. You look really . . . nice.'

I meant it. She did look nice; not at all scary, but definitely nice, which I now realised was probably how she wanted to look all along.

'Thanks,' she said, tucking a piece of hair behind her ear.

There was an awkward pause
before we both opened our mouths to
speak at exactly the same time.

'You first,' I said
quickly.

'I was just going
to say that I saw you
dancing earlier,' Evie
said. 'It looked like
you were having fun.'

'Yeah,' I said, nodding. 'I guess I was . . . How
about you? Are you having a good time?'

'Uh-huh.'

'Lola! Hurry up!'

I turned around.

Astrid and the Alices were waving me over; a
new dance circle was forming.

'Come on!' Astrid yelled.

'We need you!' Alice B added.

I was about to respond when I heard someone
yell Evie's name.

On the opposite side of the dance floor, Cleo
was standing with her hands on her hips.

For the tiniest of moments, I locked eyes with

Cleo over Evie's shoulder. I expected her to treat me to her usual smirk but she didn't, offering up a little shrug instead. Was it an apology? I wasn't sure. Either way, I knew I didn't want to fight any more.

'I should probably go,' Evie said, biting her bottom lip.

I glanced back at Astrid and the others.

'Yeah, me too.'

There was another pause. Evie took a step backwards.

'OK, well, I guess I'll see you around then?'

I nodded and took a step back of my own. 'See you around.'

Then I turned and ran over to join Astrid and the others.

'Who was that?' Alice L asked as I squeezed into the gap between her and Astrid.

I peeked over my shoulder. At that exact same moment, Evie did the same. As our eyes met, Evie gave me a small smile and wiggled her fingers in a wave. I mirrored her with a smile and wave of my own.

I turned back to Alice.

'A friend from primary school,' I replied, as Astrid grabbed my hand, whirling me round and round until I was giggling so hard, I thought I might be sick.

THE END

Lisa was born and grew up in Nottingham. She studied drama at Middlesex University and following graduation worked as an actor on stage and TV.

Between acting jobs Lisa temped in offices across London, typing stories when no one was looking, one of which eventually became her debut novel *The Art of Being Normal*. *The Art of Being Normal* has won a number of prizes including the Waterstones Children's Book Prize for Best Older Fiction 2016. Her other novels for young adults include *All About Mia*, *Paper Avalanche* and *First Day of My Life*. Lisa has also written non-fiction for younger children, including biographies of Malala Yousafzai and Dwayne 'The Rock' Johnson.

She lives in London with her husband, stepchildren and a mischievous whippet called Nelson.

Jess Bradley is an illustrator and comic artist from Torquay. As well as writing and drawing for *The Phoenix*, she also writes for *The Beano* and illustrates a variety of children's books. She has created puzzle and activity and comic books for various publishers, including the laugh-out-loud Blue Peter Award-winner, *A Day in the Life of a Poo, a Gnu and You*.

After almost deciding to become a make-up special FX artist, Jess realised that she enjoyed making comics and books a little bit more. She works from her home studio and also enjoys filling up sketchbooks with doodles of gherkins and turnips, reading and watching horror films.

Comics, cartoons and video games have been a huge influence on her work and she now gets to share her interests with her son, who beats her at most video games because she taught him too well.

Double Drama

Life isn't easy for Daniel. His mum is poorly, his dad is always working, and his five year-old twin sisters drive him up the wall! At school, he feels like he's the only kid without the latest trainers or X-Box. And worse of all, his mates are starting to notice.

When Daniel gets a starring role in the school play, he feels special for the first time in ages. But it turns out that juggling rehearsals, babysitting his sisters, and fitting in with his mates is a lot harder than it looks . . . will he get his chance to shine, or will the terrible twins ruin everything yet again?

COMING OUT IN APRIL 2024!